THE UNDERCOVER

Rock Star

BULLETPROOF

Book 1

JENNA GALICKI

Rock Star Romance with a Kick

Synopsis:

A spur-of-the-moment vacation was supposed to jolt Cameron Douglas out of his funk, but it appears he only traded locations. It was a chance meeting with a handsome stranger that changed everything. Brandon stirs Cameron's interest and his heart, but will the mysterious man reveal his true identity before their vacation in paradise is over?

Sometimes life in the spotlight was a heavy weight to bear for Brandon Bullet. He never knew if men were interested in him as a person or just enamored with his rock star status – until he meets Cameron Douglas. It wasn't often that Brandon shared a connection with someone who wasn't aware of his notoriety. He's determined to keep his identity a secret while the two of them get to know each other and before someone blows his cover.

CHAPTER ONE

A vacation was the most spontaneous thing Cameron Douglas had ever done in his life and just what he needed, but the uninhibited resort in Rio de Janeiro wasn't exactly what he had in mind. The travel agent failed to mention that his four days of serenity at the pristine beachfront hotel would be the equivalent of a nonstop wild party. Sipping a Piña Colada at the bar, he wondered when he had become a stick-in-the-mud. The answer popped into his head with little provocation – when his ex-boyfriend dumped him three months ago. The spur-of-the-moment vacation was supposed to jolt him out of his funk, but it seemed he only traded locations. He latched onto the bar in the same manner in which he bonded with his living room couch, and the remote control in his hand was replaced by a drink in a coconut husk. He was still alone and still quietly sulking.

At least the view was better. Gorgeous men were running around half naked everywhere. Movement in Cameron's shorts was a welcomed change. Although he hadn't taken a vow of celibacy since his last relationship had ended, his interest, and his sex life, had severely deteriorated.

After Cameron had his fill of the enormous taco salad in front of him, he resumed inspecting the wet, shirtless athletic gods that frolicked in the pool. A voice behind him caught his attention. He listened without turning around while the man held a short conversation with the bartender. The voice was sexy, soft, and buttery. There was grit mixed in with the friendly tone that indicated he had a hard edge, and it stirred Cameron's curiosity. He couldn't hold out any longer and needed to see the face behind the alluring voice. He spun around on the bar stool and was greeted by a pair of tattooed pecs and mauve-colored nipples that hit him at eye level. The chest they belonged to was worthy of an Olympian, and Cameron's heart just about stopped. Those gorgeous, oversized nipples were each skewered by a silver barbell and sat above a six-pack of rippled abs. Silken blond hair with a slight wave through it was knotted at the back of the man's neck. A set of broad, round shoulders were kissed with a reddish-brown hue from the sun, while the rest of his body was tanned a deep bronze. Knee-length board shorts and flip-flops were the only articles that covered his magnificent body. Two striking, aquamarine eyes stared back at Cameron, accompanied by a brilliant and charismatic smile.

"Hey." It was the only word the drop-dead gorgeous man offered.

Cameron's mouth hung open, and his mind temporarily went blank. All he could do was offer his hand in greeting. The handshake was strong, and the skin-on-skin contact sent a tingle up his arm and a flutter of excitement through his chest. He swallowed to coat his throat with saliva, and his voice returned. "Hi. I'm Cameron Douglas."

"Nice to meet you, Cameron. Can I call you Cam?"

You can call me anything you want. "Sure. No one else really does, but I can make an exception."

"What brings you to Rio during this free-for-all, Cam? You look a little out of place."

A small laugh left Cameron's throat. "Is it that obvious?"

The man placed his elbow on the bar and leaned toward Cameron with those clear blue eyes locked on his. "Let's just say, I spotted you right away."

Cameron held his breath for a brief second and questioned the innuendo in the statement. He wondered if this beautiful man was really coming on to him or if it was just his overexcited hormones twisting the guy's words. Did this hottie purposely stand next to him and make conversation with the bartender as a prelude to an introduction, or was it just a coincidence? He realized his mental conversation left a lull in the dialogue, and he quickly thought of something to fill the gap. "I told my travel agent I wanted to go somewhere fun, but I guess his idea of fun is a little different than mine."

The man's laugh was a full, rich baritone. "I know exactly how you feel. I preferred Cabo, but my buddies outvoted me on Rio." He briefly shifted his eyes toward the crowded seating area. "At least it's been a peaceful week. I leave tomorrow. It's nice to get away from the craziness sometimes and just enjoy a nice quiet day on the beach where no one knows your name."

"And what might that be?" Cameron was suddenly aware that his new crush never offered his name.

Hot Guy opened his mouth to speak, hesitated, and then brandished a broad smile. "You don't know my name?"

Cameron returned the smile with a tilt of his head. "How would I know your name? You never told me."

A questioning squint permeated one of Hot Guy's swoon-worthy eyes, and then he pressed his lips together to tone down his smile. "It's Brandon."

"Do you have a last name, Brandon?"

"I do."

"Do you want to share it?" This little guessing game was full of intrigue and coy, playful smiles.

"Last names aren't really important. Why don't we get a round of drinks and sit on the beach?" Brandon furrowed his brow with an afterthought. "Are you here alone, or did I just put my size 12 shoe in my mouth?"

Cameron let out an unexpected laugh, mainly because Brandon was wearing flip-flops, but also because of the large-foot reference. "Yes, sadly, I'm here by myself."

The broad smile returned to Brandon's handsome face. "That's not sad at all. That makes me a very happy man. What are you drinking?"

"I've been drinking these coconut things all day." Cameron picked up the empty husk and examined the remnants of the cocktail in the bottom of the shell. "But they're pushing my sugar tolerance. I'll take a beer."

Brandon raised a finger to get the attention of one of the bartenders, and one of them practically pushed the other two out of his way to take Brandon's order. This bartender was American, with a goofy smile on his face, and entirely too excited about his job. "It's a pleasure to serve you—"

"Thank you. We'll have two Coronas, please." Brandon leaned in close to the bartender and lowered his voice. "Sometimes privacy is a luxury, especially in paradise. Are there any cabanas available?"

The bartender nodded toward the beach. "Take cabana number three. I'll make sure the wait staff gets you anything you need." He placed two bottles of Corona on the bar, one in front of Brandon and the other in front of Cameron. "These are on the house. If you need anything, anything at all, just come see me. I'm happy to help you, and I'll make sure to respect your privacy."

"Thank you very much. I appreciate that." Brandon picked up his beer and clinked it against Cameron's. "Care to join me on the beach?"

Shit yeah. Hell yeah. Fuck yeah. "Sure."

As they started toward the cabana, the bartender called to Brandon. "Excuse me. Um, sir. Can you sign something for me? Uh. For the beer." He produced a blank receipt, stuffed it in a plastic tray and presented it to Brandon for his signature.

Brandon paused to read the name tag on the bartender's chest before he scribbled on the paper. Cameron peeked at the signature. He couldn't decipher Brandon's last name, but he could make out the words above it: Thanks for the brews, Andy! The interaction between Brandon and the bartender seemed odd and out of place. He studied Brandon. Confident. Charismatic. Mysterious. Twenty-something. Incredibly good looking. Sexy as fuck. He knew Brandon was hiding something. He couldn't figure out what the hell it was, nor did he care.

CHAPTER TWO

Brandon Bullet was used to blending in with the crowd when he shed his flashy wardrobe, wild hair, and black eyeliner, but he wasn't used to dodging recognition during a one-on-one conversation. The bartender clearly saw through his lackluster disguise, but Cameron Douglas was oblivious. Could it be that Cam really had no idea that he was getting hit on by the lead singer of one of America's most popular rock bands? It was a phenomenon that Brandon contemplated on their way to the beachfront.

The row of cabanas was a few yards ahead, directly facing the crystal blue ocean. Green and white striped curtains were tied to the corner posts and revealed that most of the cabanas were unoccupied. Brandon and Cam stopped in front of cabana number three and stared at its contents with an awkward pause.

Jenna Galicki

"A bed?" Cam raised an eyebrow, and his lips drew back into a sly smile.

Brandon chuckled. It couldn't have been more perfect. He put his hand to his chest to proclaim his innocence. "I had no idea."

Cam playfully rolled his eyes before he took a swig of his beer and placed it on the table next to the bed. He kicked off his flip-flops, lay down on the left side of the mattress and laced his hands behind his head. He stared up at the curtain draped across the top of the cabana without the slightest bit of unease.

Brandon joined him. They had met less than twenty minutes ago, and now they were lying next to one another, inches apart, on a bed on the beach. It was absurd and hot as hell.

Cam sighed with content. "This is nice. So, where are you from, Brandon With-No-Last-Name?"

"Fountain Valley, but I live in Los Angeles now." He assessed the dropped r's and hard consonants in Cam's speech. "Let me guess. You're from New York."

Cam smiled. "Is it that obvious?"

"Yeah. I really like that East Coast accent. It's got a hard edge that we Southern Californians can't get enough of." Brandon turned his head to face Cam. "This Southern Californian, anyway."

Cam smiled wider, shifted onto his side and propped his head up on his elbow. His warm, brown eyes twinkled like melted chocolate in the glare of the afternoon sun. "Do me a favor. Take that knot out of your hair."

Brandon stiffened, worried that recognition had finally crept into Cam's head.

"I just want to see how long it is. And touch it."

Brandon didn't need any further prompting. He sat up and unraveled the elastic that held his hair in place. His blond curls cascaded down his back and over one shoulder. The soft breeze lifted a strand and blew it across his face as he turned to see Cam's reaction.

Cam took the stray lock and tucked it behind Brandon's ear. The smile on Cam's face was full of allure and sent Brandon's heart racing. His eyes rested on Cam's gorgeous, plump lips. On any other day, with any other man, Brandon would have sucked on that bottom lip three minutes after they had met. He was waiting for the right moment to kiss Cam, and he was unsure about why he was hesitating.

"Your hair is beautiful. Why don't you wear it down?" Cam fingered the length of Brandon's hair. His hand brushed against the center of Brandon's back with a light stroke that seemed more intentional than accidental. It sent a wave of heat through Brandon's body and a tingle down his spine. Another breeze sent a lock of his hair flying, and Cam smiled. "I guess that's the reason why. I don't have that problem. I've never had my hair past my collar. What do you do for a living that allows you to wear your hair so free? I could never get away with long hair at my job. Not even in a ponytail."

The statement pretty much guaranteed that Cam had no idea about Brandon's identity. The anonymity was refreshing. Without the mark of fame, he was able to perceive Cam's interest as genuine. Brandon spent most nights surrounded by a following of handsome admirers, all competing to fuck the famous frontman of Bulletproof. He knew that most – if not all – were only interested in bedding a rock star. He never knew if anyone was really interested in him as a person. None of them probably were, since they so easily moved on to one of his bandmates. It was the downside of fame. He hated the emptiness of his mansion and the vacant half of his bed. The loneliness of single life left a void in his heart, but he could never commit to someone when he doubted their integrity.

Cam nudged Brandon's arm. "Are you dazing out on me? I asked you what you did for a living."

"I . . ." Brandon didn't have an answer to share. He wasn't ready to divulge his celebrity status, and he wasn't about to make up a fictitious occupation.

"Not going to answer that question either?" Cam, now sitting upright alongside Brandon and close enough so their thighs touched, squinted his eyes with intrigue. "You're a very elusive man. Are you going to tell me anything at all about you other than your first name?"

A waitress dressed in a short sarong and a bikini top approached the cabana and set down a bucket filled with a half dozen bottles of Corona on ice, courtesy of the bartender.

Brandon thanked her and picked up one of the ice-cold bottles. "I like beer," he said with a teasing smile.

"Me too."

"We have something in common already. Tell me more about you, and then I'll tell you a little about me." *Maybe.*

Cameron took the bottle from Brandon's hand, opened it, and handed it back to him. After he retrieved another bottle from the ice bucket for himself, he took a long sip of the brew. "I was raised in the 'burbs, but I live in Manhattan. I've been at the same boring job in Manhattan as an accountant for almost ten years. I just turned thirty. I have two sisters and a dog named Brandy." Cam lowered his gaze to his beer and picked at the label. His happy countenance turned slightly darker, and his mouth was set in a thin straight line. "I had a bad breakup a few months ago, and this weekend getaway was supposed to lift my spirits."

"Did it?"

Cam slowly smiled. "Not until you showed up." Their gaze locked on one another for a few seconds, and then Cam pointed his beer at Brandon. "Your turn."

Brandon chose his words carefully. "Well . . . I work a lot. My job forces me to travel for long periods of time, so I haven't had a long-term relationship in years." The appeal of meaningless relationships and hook-ups had diminished significantly over the last few months, and he found himself envious of those with a steady partner. "I really miss the security and intimacy of a committed relationship."

"Still avoiding the work question, I see. I'm beginning to think you're an undercover agent or something."

That was actually a great guise. "You're very clever."

"Thank you. Now tell me something else about you."

"I have a big family. Two brothers and two sisters, and my parents have been happily married for 30 years. That's a rarity where I come from."

"That's a rarity anywhere nowadays. My parents split up when I was in grade school. It took 10 years before they could be in the same room together without tearing into each other."

Brandon's thoughts drifted back to his childhood, and an incident stuck out in his head. "When I was a kid, I had this secret fear that my parents' marriage was a pretense and they were only waiting for us to grow up before they got divorced. A lot of my friends came from single-parent homes. I had always assumed that one day I would too. Once, my parents had a big fight, and I thought it was the beginning of the end." It was a sad memory that Brandon hadn't thought about in years, and he wondered why he wanted to share such an intimate detail with Cam.

"What happened?" Cam leaned closer, intent on hearing the outcome.

"They had argued for a few hours. They stormed to opposite sides of the house until they cooled off, and then they apologized to one another." Brandon shrugged. "Everything went back to normal after that, but I still thought it meant their marriage was over. I remember that I sat on pins and needles for weeks just waiting for the divorce bomb to drop, but it never came. That's when I realized I was a damn lucky kid." He was surprised by his candor. He never offered personal information about himself to people he barely knew. He was comfortable around Cam. There was no fear of shattering the illusion of Brandon Bullet, since Cam had no preconceived conceptions about him. He wanted to drop the veil of secrecy and tell Cam the truth about his stardom, but not yet. For once, he wanted to remain out of the spotlight when it came to forming a connection with someone.

Cam displayed a crooked smile. "There's so much going on in your head. I can practically hear your brain rattling. Tell me more about you. What's your favorite color? What type of music do you listen to? Who's your celebrity crush?"

Brandon laughed. "You really ask the hard questions, don't you? Favorite color: Red, like fire. Music: Hard rock." He waited for a reaction or some glint of recognition, but there was none. "Celebrity crush?" He looked off to the side and contemplated his answer before he turned to Cam with a smile. "Cameron Douglas."

Cam smiled as wide as his cheeks would allow and let out a soft chuckle. "You're really adorable."

Brandon reclined on the mattress with his hands behind his head and smiled up at the striped fabric that shielded the South American sun. "You're pretty damn adorable yourself."

Cam leaned back on one elbow and watched Brandon. They didn't say anything. They just looked into each other's eyes.

A quick rush of adrenaline filled Brandon's chest. Normally, he would have taken Cam back to his room by now, pounded the ever-loving shit out of him, and be on his way. This was a very different scenario than Brandon was used to. He didn't want to rush into sex. He wanted to get to know Cam first, even though their close proximity,

Jenna Galicki

accompanied by the fact that they were lying on a bed, made it hard for him not to think about anything except desecrating Cam's body.

A Frisbee landed on Brandon's chest, and they both let out a startled laugh at the unexpected toy.

Two girls in bikinis ran toward the cabana to retrieve the flying disc. "Sorry!" the girl in the green bikini squealed.

The girl in the yellow bikini clapped her hands and held them out toward Brandon. "Toss it back!"

Apparently, they didn't recognize Brandon either, and the undercurrent of regularity was starting to lose its appeal. They were still a good distance away, Brandon reasoned, and his appearance was grossly understated. He put his sunglasses on anyway, just as a precaution. He handed the Frisbee to Cam. "I haven't thrown one of these things since I was 16."

"You're from California and you don't know how to throw a Frisbee?" Cam asked with surprise.

Brandon shook his head.

"I play Frisbee every weekend at the park with my dog. Let me show you how it's done." He flicked his wrist, and the blue plastic disc flew right into the waiting girl's hands.

"Nice execution!" she called back. "Want to join us?" She sent a sideways glance to the girl next to her and smirked. "My friend here can't throw this thing to save her life."

That explained how it ended up on Brandon's chest.

Cam gave Brandon a teasing smile. "Think you can handle it, sunshine?" Cam pulled Brandon to his feet against his protests.

"We're going to play Frisbee? With two girls?"

"Yes." Cam dragged him through the sand by the arm. "Unless you're afraid a city boy and two girls are gonna show you up."

Now his competitive streak was aroused, to accompany his growing erection. "I was going to show you another game, back in my room."

Cam stopped and gazed over his shoulder with two smoldering eyes. "Ten minutes. Then we're outta here."

There wasn't enough room on the crowded beach to stand in a circle, so the four of them stood at the shoreline, guys against girls, with the waves gently lapping at their feet. Yellow Bikini Girl tossed the Frisbee to Cam, and he returned it with ease. Cam smiled in Brandon's direction. "Watch and learn, California boy!"

Cam and Yellow Bikini Girl seemed to be having their own private game, while Brandon and Green Bikini Girl stood useless off to the side. "Are you watching?" Cam called to Brandon, as the disc glided from his fingertips.

Brandon was watching all right – watching Cam's biceps flex, watching his calf muscles tighten, and watching Cam's firm little ass. Brandon removed his sunglasses and stuffed them into the pocket of his shorts so he could get a clearer view.

"If you two aren't going to let us play, I'm getting a drink," Green Bikini Girl complained with frustration.

Yellow Bikini Girl paused to assess her friend. "Okay. You take the forefront closest to the water, and I'll take the outside a few yards behind you." She waved directions at Brandon. "You stand in the front too, so the wind won't take the disc too far and it'll be easier for you to catch it."

Brandon sulked to the shoreline. It felt like Little League all over again.

Yellow Bikini Girl obviously knew what she was talking about, because they tossed the Frisbee back and forth a few times without decapitating anyone nearby. Oh shit. The wind took the Frisbee that was meant for Cam and blew it into a wide arc straight for Brandon. It was high above his head but rapidly descending. He trotted backwards, excitement churning in his chest at catching the Frisbee on the fly and jumped into the air with his arms stretched toward the sky. Instead of catching it, he slammed right into Cam's hard chest. He heard the air leave Cam's lungs, and they both stumbled backwards and landed in the sand.

Brandon rocked back on his butt and fell into Cam's waiting arms. He was torn between being upset that he missed catching the Frisbee and excited that he was sitting between Cam's open legs. It really was no competition. Sitting between Cam's legs was far more important – and exciting – but he acted like he was upset about the game. He twisted around so he could see Cam's face. "What happened? I almost had it."

"It was coming straight for me. You were supposed to catch the short throws."

Just like Little League – again!

They stared at each other for a moment, then erupted in laughter. Another wave inched up and drenched the sand beneath them before it receded back into the ocean, but it did little to cool the heat burning between Brandon's legs. They went from laughter to silence in an instant, and Brandon knew a kiss was about to transpire. Butterflies fluttered in his stomach, and hot passion stirred inside him. His half-closed eyes centered on Cam's mouth, and those gorgeous lips fell upon him with a heat hotter than the Brazilian sun. They consumed him, and the world around him disappeared.

When their lips parted, Cameron said, "I wanted to kiss you as soon as we started talking, but I never expected it to be like that."

"Like . . . what?" Brandon's heart thumped while he waited for Cam's answer.

"Like I can't wait to kiss you again."

Cam's lips were on Brandon in an instant. They were full and commanding, in control. Cam's tongue was soft and gentle, but it took over Brandon's mouth in a possessive display of lust. Deep warm gusts of breath were on his cheek, and he pressed his mouth hard against Cam's lips. Their bodies were so close, but they were still in an awkward, fallen-to-the-ground position, and Brandon ached for more physical contact. His hand slid around Cam's well-defined waist, noting the muscles that resided there, and he slipped the tips of his fingers under the band of Cam's shorts. He smiled under their kiss. "Let's get the hell outta here."

Cam pulled Brandon to his feet. "I never wanted to play this silly game anyway."

"Where are you two going?" Yellow Bikini Girl called after them. "We finally had a decent game going!"

They waved goodbye with a smile and walked toward the hotel.

"What floor are you on?" Cam asked when they entered the lobby.

The question left Brandon in a state of unease. How was he supposed to explain to Cam that he wasn't staying in the main hotel, and what if his unruly bandmates were around? "Do you mind if we go to your room? My friends won't give us any privacy. We're all staying together."

"Not a problem." They rode the elevator to the eighth floor, and the doors opened to a commotion in the hallway. Several maintenance men and the hotel manager were standing in front of an open door down the hall.

"What the . . .?" Cam slipped out from under Brandon's arm and walked briskly through the corridor. "That's my room!"

Brandon caught up to him just in time to hear the hotel manager's explanation. "The guests in the room upstairs left the bathtub running, and I'm afraid it flooded your room. We'll have the place cleaned up in a few hours. We're very sorry for the inconvenience. Of course, we'll be happy to comp the room for the night, but we're booked solid. We can't put you up in another room."

Cam took two steps toward the room, but never entered. He looked through the doorway and stared up at the large, wet stain on the ceiling, his eyes wide with disbelief. It was still seeping droplets of water onto the carpet. "Shit!"

Brandon inspected the damage over Cam's shoulder. It was a fucking mess. "I guess we can go to my room."

Jenna Galicki

"Are you sure? What about your friends?"

Brandon checked the time on his phone. It was still early. If he was lucky, his bandmates would be causing havoc on the streets of Brazil until early morning. He slung his arm over Cam's shoulder and escorted him back toward the elevator. "I think they'll be out for a few more hours."

Cam's finger hovered over the elevator call buttons. "Up or down?"

"Down." *Way down.*

The only other couple on the elevator stepped off on the fourth floor. Once the elevator doors closed behind them, Brandon pinned Cam against the wall. "I can't wait to get you to my room." It wasn't fair. By all rights, Brandon should be pinning Cam against the mattress right now instead of stealing a kiss in front of the security camera located on the wall of the elevator. Now, there was a good chance he would have to parade this gorgeous man in front of his horny-as-fuck bandmates who thought this week in paradise equated to a giant fuck fest.

His lips landed on Cam's mouth with urgent need. It seemed like eons since he last tasted that ravishing tongue that drove Brandon insane. It dipped into his mouth far enough to satiate Brandon's lust but not deep enough to get his fill. He pressed his hips harder against Cam, and their erections bumped into one another with a grinding friction.

The elevator dinged and the doors slowly parted at the center. Cam and Brandon quickly broke their embrace and innocently leaned their backs against the rear wall. The young couple who entered eyed them with a suspicious smile.

Cam's cat-that-ate-the-canary grin was a dead giveaway. The man couldn't summon a poker face if a million-dollar jackpot was at stake. His cheeks were flushed a warm pink, and his deep breaths were strong enough to overshadow the soft music in the elevator. At least it distracted from the erection that filled out his shorts, because a family of five could have easily sought shelter underneath the tent at his crotch.

Brandon finally dared to glance down at his own erection. Geeze! It was fucking obscene. He turned to face the wall in order to hide the monstrosity between his legs, but he misjudged the size of the thing and banged his erect cock against the wall.

He winced.

Cam smiled.

The young couple giggled.

Thankfully, freedom was only one floor away. As soon as the doors opened, Brandon took Cam's hand and led him out the back of the hotel lobby. He followed a path that was hidden between heavy greenery and hot pink bromeliads.

Cam stopped to comment on the landscaping. "These plants are beautiful. I haven't seen them on the rest of the resort." He reached out and touched one of the thick leaves and lightly fingered the stalk of the flower.

"They're bromeliads."

"How do you know that?" Cam smiled and pointed his index finger at Brandon. "You're a horticulturist?"

It made Brandon laugh. "No. Wrong again." It was his guitar player that recently had a 20-minute-long conversation with one of the landscapers about the native plants on the resort, but Brandon didn't want to explain. He took Cam's palm in his hand, and they continued walking through the lush garden.

"Where are you taking me?" Cam glanced around the out-of-the-way path. "I thought we were going to your room."

"We are. This is a shortcut."

"I'm beginning to think your room is a hammock on the beach." Cam laughed softly. "I'm game if you are."

There was a hammock . . . and a hot tub, and a pool table, and a full bar. He had no idea how to explain that his room was really a private, four-bedroom villa that sat only steps from the ocean. They came to the end of the path which opened up to a secluded area of the resort. There were only five villas on the beautiful, unblemished shoreline. Bulletproof occupied the second villa from the end, and as far as Brandon could see, all seemed quiet – for the moment.

Cam's jaw fell open when he realized that Brandon was leading him to the doorstep of one of the grand villas. "This is where you're staying?"

"I prefer to maintain a low profile when we travel. I would have been happy with a suite on one of the top floors, but my friends are a little extravagant." Brandon swiped his card in the slot, and they stepped inside.

Cam inspected the open floor plan in awe. His eyes darted from the fireplace to the pool table, then drifted into the dining room and through the alcove that led to the kitchen. His gaze settled on the stairs that led to the second level before he turned to Brandon. "How the hell can you afford to stay in a place like this? Who the fuck *are* you?"

"I'm just a guy who wants to get to know you better. Does it really matter why I can afford to stay in a villa with my friends?" Eventually he would tell Cam that he was a famous musician, but he wanted to live the fantasy of being just a regular guy a little longer. It had been years since he slept with someone who only thought of him as "Brandon Bullet, human being" and not "Brandon Bullet, rock star."

Brandon took two bottles of water from the mini fridge under the bar. "I have a feeling we're going to be pretty thirsty in about an hour."

"An hour? That's it?" Cam teased. "I would have thought Mr. Rich-and-Famous would give me a full night of never-ending passion." He motioned to the expansive villa. "I thought you'd live up to your reputation."

Brandon's smile waned, and his heart was suddenly heavy. He was hoping to hide from the pressure of notoriety, but even with his identity concealed, the shadow of wealth and fame held him in its realm. It was a bar that he was constantly trying to hurdle. While he contemplated his dual personalities with frustration, he found himself in Cam's warm embrace.

"I was kidding." Cam's voice was soothing and sincere. "I don't care that you're rich or who your friends are. I'm here because I want to be with you – Brandon Whatever-Your-Last-Name-Is." Cam's soft lips landed on Brandon's mouth. "I love the mystery behind your identity, but promise me that before you leave this resort, you'll tell me everything. I'd hate to spend the rest of my life wondering about you."

"I will. Just not right now. Right now, I want to do this." Brandon kissed Cam with all the pent-up passion in his heart. One hand traveled over Cam's strong shoulder and caressed the curve of Cam's bicep, while the other hand slid around Cam's taut waist, and his hand cupped one cheek of the finest ass in South America.

The temperature in the room rose several degrees as the heat between them escalated. Brandon needed to possess this man before he exploded. He tried to break the kiss so he could move things upstairs, but Cam wouldn't part with his lips. Cam was stronger than he looked, and he wouldn't let Brandon out of his embrace or release the kiss. Cam definitely wasn't a submissive man, and Brandon started to wonder about the dynamics of their love making. Brandon wasn't a bottom, but he might be for Cam. He struggled to break free, but Cam refused to remove his lips. Did the man ever breathe?

Air suddenly seemed unnecessary. The aroma of Cam's body, mixed with the tiny bit of sweat from their day in the sun, provided the only sustenance Brandon needed to survive. He inhaled deeply, allowing the intoxicating fragrance to fill his nostrils and feed his lungs.

Cam finally took a breath. "Where's your room?"

Brandon led them up the stairs to the second floor of the villa. Without Cam in his direct line of sight, he was unable to keep his focus straight ahead and turned back to look over his shoulder every few steps. Cam had his eyes permanently fixated on the back of Brandon's shorts, and it sent a rumbling through Brandon's crotch. It was more than just the usual excitement that preceded sex. He was filled with a fresh sense of self-worth, and it was the ultimate turn-on.

Cam cupped one side of Brandon's ass in the palm of his hand when they made it to the landing and gave it a healthy squeeze. "Do you know how close I came to biting this thing on the way up the stairs?"

Images of Cam's teeth on Brandon's body made him abruptly stop walking. He pushed Cam against the wall, gave him one mouth-watering kiss, then pulled him toward the bedroom before they ended up naked on the floor in the hallway.

As soon as the door was closed, he placed both hands on either side of Cam's face and gave him an aggressive kiss. Cam pushed back with equal passion and vigor. It was exhilarating and challenging to be with a forceful man instead of one who succumbed to Brandon's social status.

He tugged Cam's shirt over his head and threw it to the floor, revealing a well-defined chest and lean torso. Cam responded by pulling Brandon's shorts down, so they fell to his ankles. It was another act of defiance, and he met Cam's stare with an erotic smile. "Are you going to try to take the upper hand all night, Mr. Douglas?"

Cam flattened Brandon against the wall and pressed his full weight against him. "I always take the upper hand."

A hot jolt of electricity soared through Brandon's body. He wasn't used to such aggression, and it revved his testosterone level into high gear. He stepped out of his shorts, which were still pooled around his ankles, spun Cam around so their positions were reversed, and pinned Cam's hands above his head. "We may just have to fight it out for the top."

"I'm always on top." There was playful defiance in Cam's eyes. "Do you think you can make me submit?"

Brandon's blood pumped harder in his chest. His previous lovers were entirely too easy to dominate. "Do you think I can break you?"

Cam wiggled out from under Brandon's hold and grabbed Brandon's forearms with a strong grip. Now in control, he pushed Brandon backwards toward the bed. They both fell onto the mattress with a laugh, but Cam maintained a hold on Brandon's wrists and landed on top. Brandon struggled in an erotic test of wills and strength and flipped Cam onto his back. He straddled Cam and immobilized his hands on the mattress.

"You're pretty strong." Cam raised his brow with surprise and displayed a sinister grin. "But not strong enough." They playfully wrestled on top of the bed and rolled over several times, each vying for top position. Their playful wrestling game was a seductive display of power. Laughter punctuated their antics. When they finally came to rest, Brandon was flat on the bed with Cam seated across his thighs and his hands held captive in Cam's tight grip. Panting from exertion and laughter, Brandon surrendered and stopped struggling. A moment of intense sexual passion passed between them as they held each other's gaze.

Cam slowly loosened his hold on Brandon's wrists and dusted his fingertips over Brandon's chest and around his waist. He found

Brandon's erection and held it in the palm of his hand. "Does this mean I get to be on top?"

"I guess it does. You won." Brandon nodded toward his cock. "And that's your prize."

Cam's lips came down on Brandon's with a suffocating heat. Even though he lost their little tussling match, Brandon wasn't relinquishing command so easily. He still fought for control and tried to roll Cam onto his back, but Cam only pressed his lips down harder. Brandon pushed his fingers through Cam's short, bristly hair and held his head in place while he dominated their kiss. He tried to overpower Cam's tongue and flicked it with authority, then changed its movement to a heavy swirl. Every time his tongue changed direction, Cam followed. Just when Brandon was satisfied that he had the upper hand on their kiss and still maintained some sort of hierarchy, Cam broke the kiss and sunk his teeth into Brandon's neck. Brandon gasped and dug his fingers into the fleshy slabs of Cam's butt cheeks and gyrated his hips in a circle.

The moment he felt Cam's body relax, Brandon seized the upper hand and rolled Cam onto his back. He was surprised at the lack of resistance. He paused for a moment to take in the pleasurable contours of Cam's physique. He ran his hands over Cam's pecs and across his tight abs, then kissed each one. He pulled Cam's shorts down to his knees, and a long hard cock landed in Brandon's mouth, exactly where he wanted it. Brandon sucked and tickled the head of Cam's cock with his tongue. He circled the shaft with the fingers of one hand while the other hand gently cupped and massaged Cam's delicate scrotum. Cam's balls were smooth and robust and a beautiful shade of pink.

Cam let out a long, animalistic moan and kicked off his shorts. He extended his hips upwards and offered himself deeper into Brandon's mouth. Brandon licked the shaft, circled the head, and traced a trail down to Cam's sac with his tongue. He sucked one testicle into his mouth, and then the other. Cam gasped and grunted with pleasure and surprise. Brandon lifted Cam's hips off the bed and spread his cheeks so he could see Cam's sweet little hole. It puckered with invitation. Brandon wanted to taste it and he flicked his tongue against the opening and poked it inside. Cam's scent was intoxicating, and he tasted like a forbidden candy. Brandon sucked on his index finger to lubricate it, then dipped the tip inside Cam's bottom just past the rim and deep enough to make Cam gasp.

"Oh, God! That feels so fucking good!"

A satisfied smile spread across Brandon's face. If his plan worked, Cam would be begging for penetration in about three minutes. He had a distinct feeling that Cam's aggression was more posturing than dominance, and he wanted to tease Cam into submission.

Brandon's finger continued its relentless attack against the hard muscles inside Cam's bottom. He took Cam's swollen cock into his mouth until it hit the back of his throat. He moved his mouth in perfect conjunction with his finger to accelerate the mounting pleasure.

Cam panted heavily and rocked Brandon's head back and forth by a handful of his hair. Cam spread his legs wider and moved a pillow under his hips to afford viable access. He moaned and sighed. "Your mouth is perfect. Your finger is teasing the fuck out of me. Put it inside. Deeper. Please. Put two fingers inside me. Put your whole goddamn hand in there."

Brandon smiled around Cam's cock. Those were the words he wanted to hear. With a dollop of lube from the bottle in the drawer of the bedside table, Brandon inserted one finger in Cam's bottom until it disappeared. Cam moaned and pulled his knees up, so his hole opened wider. A second finger joined the first with little resistance. Brandon licked and sucked Cam's cock in tune to the movement of his fingers. In. Out. Then back in with a circular motion. Cam was grunting and ready to explode. That's when Brandon backed off. He slowly withdrew his fingers, then his mouth, and set Cam's protesting cock free with a wet pop.

Cam jerked his head up. "Don't stop."

Brandon crawled up Cam's body and placed a hard kiss on his lips. "Tell me you want it, Cam. Because I can give it to you. Real good. My cock can bring you to ecstasy and back. Let me be on top."

Mischief lit up Cam's eyes. "I would have let you top the minute you pinned me against the wall. I just loved the power game we played."

A provocative laugh floated from Brandon's mouth. "You little cock tease. So, you're a bottom after all."

"I'm versatile."

Brandon put his lips to Cam's ear. "Good, because I'm going to fuck you senseless."

Cam responded by flipping Brandon onto his back and straddling him. "You'd better. But first, I'm gonna suck you off until you cry like a little girl."

The sudden burst of aggression gave Brandon a rush. Cam's constant challenge for control aroused his body and his mind to new heights.

Cam's lips covered Brandon's mouth, and then he ravaged Brandon's chest with hungry kisses. His tongue traced a wet line down the center of Brandon's chest and nursed on his nipples. He nibbled on the barbells and tugged harshly on them with his teeth. "I wanted to bite these enormous nipples of yours the moment I turned around on the barstool."

His words sent Brandon into a writhing mess. He lifted his hips, gyrated his pelvis against Cam's abdomen, and let out a long moan. "Show me what else your mouth can do."

Cam licked a path across Brandon's abs and outlined each muscle with his tongue. He licked a straight line down past Brandon's navel to the base of his cock. Cam nipped and sucked a tender spot on Brandon's lower abdomen, close enough so that Brandon's cock rested against his cheek. Cam's teeth clamped down on the delicate flesh with a force that made Brandon's shoulders rise off the mattress. While Cam's teeth bore down, he sucked the flesh into his mouth and soothed it with his tongue. It brought both pain and pleasure in equal amounts.

Brandon whimpered and ran his fingers through Cam's short hair. "You're torturing me. You're driving me fucking crazy."

It was obviously Cam's intent, and he smiled against Brandon's abdomen. He purposely brushed the tip of Brandon's engorged cock against his cheek every time he stroked it. He abandoned the purple prize he bestowed on Brandon's abdomen and placed the tip of Brandon's cock in his mouth. He teased it with a gentle flick of his tongue across the slit and around the head while his hand kept a steady stroke up and down the shaft.

Cam sucked him so hard he almost came the moment Cam's mouth engulfed him. While Cam's mouth performed a powerful suction, his hand gripped Brandon's cock firmly around the base. His strong hand followed his lips up and down the shaft so that every inch of Brandon's cock was stimulated. Cam's other hand found Brandon's sac and roughly massaged his balls. It was a tiny bit painful, but the unyielding pleasure far outweighed the discomfort.

Brandon's nerve endings were on fire. He had never experienced such a well-executed blowjob before. Cam's mouth was divine. He shuddered and let out a long moan. "Stop," he whispered. "You need to stop before I come." Cam slowed and some of the tingling subsided just enough for Brandon to stifle the orgasm that threatened to drown him. As soon as his breathing regulated, Cam's mouth resumed its never-ending assault. "Oh, God!" Brandon whimpered, and he grabbed a chunk of Cam's hair. "Stop. Please stop so I can fuck you. Please!"

Cam kissed his way up Brandon's body and placed a sensual kiss on his lips. Then he rolled onto the bed next to Brandon. "I'm ready."

Jenna Galicki

Brandon jumped on top of Cam and gave him a hard kiss. He quickly bathed his fingers in lube and found Cam's hole. He worked two fingers inside while his tongue licked Cam's cock.

Cam was flailing on the mattress and heaving heavy breaths. He picked his knees up and repositioned the pillow under his hips. "Hurry up and fuck me, because I'm an impatient man. I need you inside me."

Mr. Bottom was mouthy, and Brandon gave him a gentle nip on his ball sac to remind him who was in charge. Cam jerked and his legs stiffened, then he relaxed and let out a deep breath. He submitted, which meant he trusted Brandon. It probably wasn't easy for a dominant bottom like Cam to relinquish power. Brandon removed his fingers, wiped them on the sheet, and found a condom waiting for him. Cam had retrieved it from the bedside table. Brandon kissed Cam with assurance and tenderness, and a moment of mutual respect passed between them.

Brandon was about to tear open the condom, but Cam took him by the wrists and pulled him into a sitting position with his legs hanging over the side of the mattress. Brandon smiled. Even though Cam was going to bottom, he was still taking the lead.

Cam took the condom, tore open the package with his teeth, and rolled it onto Brandon's cock. He was so over-stimulated that he almost exploded when he watched Cam bend over, spread his butt cheeks and smother his hole with lube.

Cam put his mouth to Brandon's ear. "You'd better hold onto something, because I'm gonna bottom you so fucking hard."

Brandon sucked in a deep breath. He had no doubt it was going to be the ride of his life.

Cam turned, squatted over Brandon's cock, and waited for the proper alignment. Brandon placed one hand on Cam's beautiful, cream-colored butt cheek and nudged his cock against Cam's hole. Cam let out a deep breath and bore down with his hips. He threw his head back and braced his hands on his knees. Cam was tight and his muscles squeezed Brandon's cock as he pushed deeper. Cam never slowed, even though Brandon knew he was struggling with the girth.

"That's it," Brandon coaxed. "Take it all, baby."

Cam moaned with one final push, and his butt landed on Brandon's lap with his cock buried deep inside. Cam lifted his hips up and down, grunting loudly with each repetition. He picked up speed until his cheeks were slamming into Brandon's hip bones. Their balls smashed together repeatedly with a hard bounce, but it was an erotic pain that felt so fucking good. Brandon held onto Cam's hips to propel his momentum and encouraged him. "That's it, Cam. Oh God. You're a fucking animal."

Brandon's words spurred Cam's drive, and he thrust harder. The bed shook, and the headboard banged against the wall with a series of loud thuds. Faster. Harder. Deeper. Brandon could barely catch his breath.

Cam started stroking his cock to the same rhythm of his hips, and then increased his tempo dramatically. "Are you ready?" His teeth were clenched so tightly that his words were muffled and distorted.

"Uh. Huh." Brandon was breathing too hard to make a coherent sentence. Stimulation pulsed through his cock, down into his sac, and shot through his legs. He stiffened, leaned back on his elbows, lifted his pelvis and bowed his body into a perfect arc. Cam propelled himself harder with each backwards thrust and emitted loud, long grunts. Brandon convulsed underneath him and came with a silent gasp of breath that left him dizzy.

Cam shuddered. The muscles in his thighs twitched from fatigue, and he leaned all of his weight onto Brandon's still-arced legs. All of Brandon's strength vanished, and he collapsed underneath Cam. They both fell back onto the bed and slid to the floor with the satiny sheets beneath them.

Cameron struggled to catch his breath. He hadn't power bottomed in a long time, and God, it felt awesome! He tumbled out of Brandon's arms and brushed the hair off of Brandon's face so that he could see the gorgeous blue of his eyes.

Brandon lay limp on the floor, with his arms stretched to his sides, but managed a broad smile. "I thought I was supposed to fuck you. Are you a control freak, or are you just trying to kill me?"

A deep, erotic laugh flew from Cameron's mouth. "I told you to hold onto something." He sprung to his feet and pulled Brandon up and onto the bed. He opened a bottle of water, guzzled half of its contents, and handed the rest to Brandon. Beads of sweat glistened off the mounds of Brandon's chest, and his spectacular abs sparkled. They were six tiny mountains of magnificence.

Jenna Galicki

He opened the French doors to the balcony to let the fresh air in and was greeted by the setting sun. It cast a warm glow over the ocean's horizon and on the sand.

Cameron returned to his lover's bed with a contented heart. The salted air blew into the room and lifted the hair off of Brandon's shoulders with a light bounce. His blond locks were tousled around his face in turbulent waves from their wild love making and formed a golden silhouette. It was much sexier than the neat little knot.

Cameron sat on the edge of the bed and stared into the eyes of his mysterious lover. The weekend that he thought was a waste of time and money had turned into one night of sheer heaven. Brandon pulled him in for a kiss, and it fed the fire that was still burning inside him. He couldn't remember the last time he felt such an intense attraction to another man. A warm gust of ocean air hit Cameron's naked back and sent a fresh shiver up his back. "Let's sit on the balcony."

Brandon reached for Cameron's cheek. "Why didn't I meet you five days ago?"

"Because I was in New York sitting behind my desk in a stuffy office building." He slipped on his briefs and tossed Brandon his shorts. Loud voices and laughter from the beach caught his attention. "Sounds like someone's having a good time out there." He crossed the room and stood at the railing of the balcony. The voices belonged to a large group by the shore enjoying a bonfire.

"Don't pay attention to them." Brandon wrapped his arms around Cameron's waist from behind and placed a kiss on the back of his neck. They squeezed into the comfy lounge chair together and faced the ocean. The gentle waves crashed into the sand and created a tranquility of white noise, while the sun turned the sky a dark magenta. They embraced in a serene hug while Cameron rested his head on Brandon's tanned shoulder and sighed. Thoughts of Brandon's departure weighed heavily on his heart. He wanted more time together. He wanted to know Brandon's history, his present-day story and what his future held, but time wasn't on their side. "What time are you leaving tomorrow?"

"Early." Brandon sighed. "In a few hours, actually. We head out around 5:30 in the morning."

Cameron's heart dropped into the pit of his stomach. "I was hoping we could have breakfast in the morning, before your flight. I didn't realize you were leaving so early."

"Stay with me tonight." Brandon placed a delicate kiss on Cameron's lips. "I want to take advantage of every minute we have left together."

"I'd like that." Warmth spread through Cameron's chest at the mutual sentiment. He hadn't been exactly sure what the elusive man in his arms was thinking half the time. Now he knew they shared the same connection, and it filled him with joy.

"I want this to be more than a hook-up, Cam. I'm more attracted to you than I've been to anyone in a long time." Sadness seeped into Brandon's soft blue eyes, and they lost some of their light. "But I know that's not possible when we live thousands of miles apart. I travel a lot, so I know I'll make it to New York at some point, and I hope we can see each other again. I know it's unrealistic to make expectations, but I'd like to know that it's an option."

Cameron tried to remain optimistic, but he was a realist. Good intentions were sincere, but time and distance pushed memories to the wayside. "I know the statistics. We'll both go our separate ways and meet other people once we're back in the real world." Although Cameron's heart felt like it was just kicked to its core, he maintained a soft smile on his face. "I'd like to keep an open mind though. Anything's possible."

Brandon tightened his arms around Cameron in a possessive embrace. "Good. Because I don't want this to be over yet."

Voices from the beach grew steadily louder – the same voices from the bonfire – until they sounded like they were right outside the villa. A door slammed downstairs, and the voices were now clearly audible from the living room. "Those were your friends on the beach?"

Brandon nodded.

"Why didn't you say anything?"

"Because I knew that once they came back here, you'd find out who I really am." He took a deep breath that was filled with trepidation. "I'm Brandon Bullet, lead singer for Bulletproof."

"You're in a band?" Cameron listened to news radio. He wasn't up to date on the latest music, and he prodded his memory for recognition. "I don't think I've heard of Bulletproof."

Brandon laughed with surprise, and his anxiety disappeared. "Are you serious? I was hiding my identity from you, so I'd know you cared about me as a person, not the rock star image, and you've never even heard of my band?"

"I'm not—" Music burst through the villa at an unheard-of decibel, and Cameron recoiled from the loud noise.

Brandon dropped his chin into his chest and displayed a sheepish smile. "Sorry. My bandmates don't know how to turn down their amps. I scream my head off half the time just to be heard over their music. Plus, that's kinda my thing."

It was still sinking into Cam's head that Brandon was a rock star when someone yelled up the stairs.

"Hey, Brandon! We know you're up there! Get down here! We need our singer!"

"Yeah," another voice yelled. "Or else Jeremy's gonna sing and then every dog in the neighborhood is gonna start howling."

"Shut up, asshole!" a third voice replied.

Brandon rolled his eyes with affection. "Those are my bandmates, which explains why I didn't want you to meet them. I love them like brothers, but they kid around like teenagers." His expression turned serious, and tiny lines appeared between his brows. "I'm sorry I didn't tell you. I just wanted you to like me for me. Sometimes it's hard to know who to trust and who to believe. I liked that you didn't know I was famous."

The hint of vulnerability took Cameron by surprise, and his heart went out to Brandon. "You're still the same guy I met this afternoon. You're no different than you were ten minutes ago."

Someone pounded on the bedroom door. "Get your ass downstairs, Bran!"

"All right!" Brandon groaned. "I'll be down in a minute." He gave Cameron an apologetic tilt of his head. "Do you mind?"

"No. I'd love to hear you sing."

"Thanks for understanding. Put some clothes on first. I don't trust my horny bandmates around you."

The living room was littered with an entourage of people. They were mostly men – very good-looking men – who seemed to have lost their shirts. A small crowd surrounded Brandon as soon as he made it to the bottom of the stairs. He politely said hello and continued through the crowd without letting go of Cameron's hand.

A tattooed guitarist sat on the arm of the couch and produced an ear-splitting wail from the small amp at his feet. The other arm of the couch was occupied by the bassist, thumping out a low rumble. In the corner of the room, three guys were setting up a drum set at lightning speed.

Brandon motioned to the room full of people. "Just another ordinary night with Bulletproof. Welcome to my world."

Cameron stood back and took it all in – the excitement, the gorgeous men, the beautiful girls, the bottles of champagne, and the general stimulation that buzzed in the room. It was electrifying. He was left flabbergasted, without words to verbalize the merriment around him.

The drummer sat behind his kit and added a beat to the guitar and bass, and a song came to life. Someone thrusted a mic in Brandon's hand, and he looked at it with apprehension. He put his lips to

Cameron's ear so he could be heard over the music. "Are you sure you don't mind?"

The room was filled with energy and Cameron's heart pounded in his chest along with the music. He was thrilled at the opportunity to hear Brandon sing with his band and to be part of the impromptu concert happening before him. "I'm looking forward to it, Brandon. I'd be disappointed if you didn't."

Brandon boasted a proud smile, and he gave Cameron a small kiss. "Thank you." An aura washed over Brandon as he morphed into a rock star. He ran his fingers through his hair and shook it, so it was wild and free. He rolled his shoulders, stuck out his bare chest and stood taller.

Brandon brought the mic to his lips and sang with a gritty, sexy rasp that stirred Cameron's insides and brought his erection back to life. Every pair of eyes were on Brandon as he moved through the crowd, but his gaze kept returning to Cameron. They shared a connection that a room full of people couldn't break.

Cameron watched Brandon with adoration and longing tugged at his heart. He craved more than one night with the hot, sexy singer.

When the song was over, the room erupted into a round of applause and cheers, and Brandon made his way back to Cameron's side.

"That was incredible! But why did you stop?" Cameron motioned to the enthusiastic crowd. "Everyone wants to hear you sing."

Brandon covered the mic with his hand and lowered it to his side. "What do you want? These guys could keep me here all night."

"I want to hear you sing." Cameron smiled lovingly. He was filled with an incredible rush of adrenaline and pride. "Not all night, but a few more songs." He slipped his hands behind Brandon's neck. "I still want you to myself before the sun comes up."

Brandon pulled him in for a deep kiss. He could feel Brandon's heart beating against his chest, and it made Cameron's blood pump faster. Someone in the room let out a whistle, probably one of Brandon's lively band members, and they both smiled with their lips still pressed against one another.

Thirty minutes later, Brandon finished his brief set. He gulped a half bottle of water and took Cameron's hand. "I want to introduce you to my bandmates." He brought Cameron to the guitar player first. "This is Derek, my closest friend and the biggest pain in my ass."

Derek shook Cameron's hand. "Don't believe anything this guy says about me." He and Brandon exchanged a brief glance, and Cameron saw the close bond of their friendship. "We were wondering what the hell happened to Brandon today. Now I can understand why he stood us up."

"I'm afraid I kidnapped him the moment I saw him," Cameron answered. "I couldn't help myself."

The bass player bumped Derek out of the way. "I'm Jeremy. Feel free to tie me up and kidnap me anytime."

"Stay the hell away from this guy," Brandon winked at Cameron, then gave Jeremy a good-natured shove. He pointed to the drummer who already had a lip-lock on a fair-haired twink. "That's Alan, but he looks kind of busy. Hey, Alan, can you come up for air long enough to say hello to my friend Cam?"

Alan held the twink's face steady, lifted his head long enough to say, "Hello, Cam," then resumed his make-out session.

"Hello," Cameron waved.

"That's my crazy-ass band. Now that you've met them, let's go someplace private."

Cameron took one last glance around the villa. It was filled with lively faces, tossing back drinks. There was a vivacious energy and a contagious excitement that ignited Cameron's soul. This was probably a routine evening for Brandon, and it made Cameron realize what an utterly mundane and boring life he led.

"You look like you want to stay."

Cameron slowly turned his head toward Brandon and smiled. "Not a fucking chance."

"Good." They joined hands and walked to the shore. The night had cooled, but there was a warm, humid breeze that made the air perfect for a walk along the oceanfront. The live music was still audible from the villa, minus Bulletproof's lead singer. Cameron looked toward the revelry at the villa and imagined their disappointment when he whisked Brandon away. *Sorry, folks. You can have him every other night of the year. Tonight, he's mine.*

"We can head back in a little while, if you want."

Cameron turned away from the villa and returned his attention to the man at his side. "No. I want you all to myself." He received the warmest smile in reply, which made his heart jump. "I was just remembering how excited those people were to see you, and what it must be like for them to be at an unexpected beach party in Rio de Janeiro with a famous rock band."

"I can't say for sure what it's like for them, but I loved it. They looked like they were having a good time too. That's all that matters – that the fans enjoy the show and the music."

"You're just a glutton for the attention, huh?" Cameron gave Brandon a playful poke in the ribs, and his finger met a set of rigid abs.

Brandon let out a short laugh. "I'm not gonna lie. I do enjoy it."

Cameron couldn't imagine what it was like to be the center of attention in front of so many people. He was way too introverted for that kind of public display. "What is it like for you on stage? How does it feel to be up there in front of tens of thousands of people?"

Brandon looked into the distance and his eyes took on a hypnotic stare. "It's like . . . a dream. There's nothing like it in the world. The energy of the crowd is a physical presence that I feel all over my body." He shuddered, slightly. "It's surreal. I feed off the shouts and screams from the people in the audience. We're connected. Their voices are a line that ties us together. It's me and them. And my band of course. Me and Alan and Jeremy and Derek are one and the same up on that stage. Performing without them would be like the world with no color. The music they create lights up my soul."

The way Brandon described it left Cameron with a sense of wonder, and he yearned for something – anything – of the same caliber in his life.

They came to a long pier that extended over the ocean. They both gravitated toward it at the same time, exchanging a small smile at

Jenna Galicki

their unspoken decision to walk onto the pier. It was a good 30 feet long, and they walked to the end. At this point, the beautiful clear, blue water took on a dark hue from the night sky. There were a million stars above, and the moonlight reflected off the ocean's surface like a mirror. It was beautiful.

Brandon kicked off his sneakers and pulled his shirt over his head. Cameron watched the brilliant muscles of the rock star's chest and shoulders, which shimmered from the flecks of light bouncing off the water. Brandon's jeans and underwear dropped to his ankles, and he stepped out of them.

This gorgeous man stood in front of Cameron completely naked, and it made his cock swell. He took a step forward, grabbed Brandon by the waist and pulled him in for a powerful kiss. Those fleshy lips pushed back with just the right amount of pressure, and it sent a wave of adrenaline through Cameron's veins. His heart was galloping in his chest so hard he could hear it between his ears. He didn't really care that they were still on the hard, wooden pier. He'd endure a few splinters for another round with Brandon Bullet, but he'd much rather prefer the softness of the sand. He broke the kiss and impatiently shed his clothes.

A pair of strong, controlling hands landed on either side of Cameron's cheeks and held him in place while his lips were assaulted with another hard kiss. He grabbed onto Brandon's wrists and straightened his shoulders. Leaning forward, he dominated the kiss with a hefty swirl of his tongue.

Brandon suddenly pulled away in order to take a deep gust of breath. "Your touch. Your kiss. You light my body on fire."

"Ditto, rock star." Cameron glanced down at the pier, then grabbed a nice handful of Brandon's butt and squeezed it. "Do you want to move to the sand, so I don't have to pick splinters out of this sweet ass?"

Brandon challenged him with a raised brow and teasing smile. "You mean, so I don't have to pick splinters out of *your* ass."

Cameron chuckled and chose not to go head to head. He had better things in mind. "OK," he conceded. "We'll pick splinters out of each other's ass."

"Actually, I undressed because I was going for a swim. You're the one who accosted my body and started this."

A swim? Cameron's hard-on quickly deflated. He hated the water and never ventured in past his knees.

"Come on." Brandon took Cameron's hand and led him the last few feet to the edge of the pier. "Let's have a quick swim first, then we can flip a coin to see who pulls what out of whose ass."

Every fiber in Cameron's body was resisting and his heartrate was skyrocketing, but his feet followed Brandon. What in the hell was he getting himself into? While he was trying to think of a way to steer them away from the water, Brandon dove in.

The slender arc of Brandon's form pierced the water with a minimal splash, and he was lost beneath the opaque blackness. Cameron stood at the end of the last plank with his toes hanging over the edge. He counted the seconds since he last saw Brandon: one . . . two . . . three . . . four. With the grace of someone well acquainted with the water,

Brandon's head popped up and his arms gently stirred circles in the ocean's surface.

"What are you waiting for, Cam? The water is beautiful!" Brandon disappeared again under the water. His adorable pale butt cheeks surfaced for a brief moment, like a dolphin's back peeking through the surf, before it was gone leaving the water still against the dark horizon. Brandon reappeared again, this time closer to the pier. "Do I have to come up there and throw you in?"

It was a tempting offer. The idea of struggling with Brandon sounded like the perfect prelude to some feisty foreplay, but Cameron didn't want to end up tossed into the water. If he was going in, it would be of his own volition. He lacked the assurance to just dive in the way Brandon had. Instead, he sat on the edge of the pier and prepared himself to gently slip into the water, but Brandon called out to him.

"Hey, city boy! You're gonna get a sac full of splinters sliding off the edge like that. Stand up and jump in! Unless you want me to poke around your balls with a pair of tweezers." Brandon's white smile shone brightly in the shadows below.

"Very funny!" Cameron got to his feet. He did a series of stretches, really just to psyche himself up for the plunge, but thought it would be a nice teasing gesture to pay Brandon back for making him take a midnight swim. He let out a deep breath – now or never – and gave a half-hearted leap off the pier. He landed feet first in the water without going under and hoped it didn't make him look like a total dork. He wasn't a swimmer but was able to tread water. It was surprisingly warm and pleasant, but he still felt the need to glance around every few seconds. After all, this was prime shark-bait time.

Brandon waded closer and offered a kiss. His mouth was as warm as the ocean and Cameron could taste its salty flavor. It was inviting and sexy to feel the water sway between their bodies. Then the kiss became aggressive, and Cameron didn't have the skill to stay afloat and assert a dominant posture at the same time, and he sank a little lower in the water. Momentarily panicked, he wrapped his arms and legs around Brandon.

Pushed off balance by the surprise added weight, Brandon kicked his legs and flapped his arms under the water for a moment before regaining his stature. He was incredibly adept in the water and supported both of them with little effort. "So, you're trying to drown me now?"

"No. I just had a sudden urge to be closer to you." He still had his arms and legs wrapped around Brandon. "I just thought that with the buoyancy of the water you'd be able to handle my body weight. But if I'm too heavy . . ." He started to paddle away, but Brandon pulled him back.

"Get back here, wise guy." Brandon took hold of Cameron by the wrists and pulled his arms around his neck. The warm water splashed between them as their bodies pressed together. Cameron locked his ankles around Brandon's back, and they bobbed there in the silence of the night. The sexual overtones that they had shared all day now turned to quiet intimacy. They were naked against one another under the water, but the connection was more than just sexual. It was an exchange of deep affection for one another.

Brandon placed a gentle kiss on Cameron's lips. The invasive tongue was filled with passion, but the take-charge and controlling attitude that Brandon had exhibited all night was reduced to a tender rotation of his mouth. It was so delicate and different from their lust-filled aggressive kisses, but it was just as hot, and Cameron loved this new, less-dominant side of Brandon.

The villa was a miniature version of itself in the distance, reminding Cameron of how far out into the ocean they were. The shark phobia had drastically abated. His heart no longer thudded in his chest, and the need to constantly monitor his surroundings was satisfied by a mere glance at the water's surface every now and then.

A slight breeze picked up and Cameron shuddered.

"We should get back," Brandon said. "My fingers are starting to prune. He ran a wet hand over Cameron's shoulder. "And you have goosebumps."

"It's getting chilly." Cameron reluctantly released his hold on Brandon and paddled a few feet away to the ladder that led up to the pier. As he climbed the rungs and ascended higher, the cool air nipped at his naked body. A wet slap on his ass sent a small fire across his right butt cheek, and he jumped onto the pier. He laughed down at Brandon and offered his hand.

Brandon took it and stepped onto the pier. He pulled Cameron into him, and their chests bumped together with a hard slap.

Cameron took a chunk of Brandon's ass in his hand and gave it a nice, healthy squeeze just as the wind whipped passed them. A shiver ran down his back, and he leaned his face into Brandon's shoulder.

"You're cold." Brandon's voice turned gentle with concern, and he ran his hand up and down the length of Cameron's arm to generate heat.

"You're warm." Cameron pressed his body against Brandon's to absorb some of the heat coming from the man.

"Come on. Let's get you dry." Brandon scooped up their clothing, took Cameron by the hand and led him down the pier and back onto the sand. He started running and Cameron followed. It was twice as cold now that they picked up speed, and laughter flew from Cameron's mouth as he ran.

They stopped at a line of hammocks midway between the villas and the shore. There was a stack of beach towels in a cubby next to each hammock, and Brandon tossed a large towel to Cameron. With one towel draped over his shoulders, Brandon quickly dried his hair with another.

Watching Brandon's muscles flex with the rough movements of his arms and shoulders made Cameron completely forget about the cold. He stood with the towel poised across his back and stared at the tattoos that shimmered across Brandon's chest and the wild mane of wet hair that was tousled around Brandon's handsome face.

Brandon stopped when he saw Cameron watching him. He walked toward him with the outstretched towel and surrounded him with

Jenna Galicki

it. It was a warm, fluffy embrace of soft cotton, but Brandon was left out, exposed to the cool ocean breeze.

"Get in here." Cameron snaked his hands through the slice where the ends of the towel met and invited Brandon inside. It wasn't big enough to completely envelop both of them and a section of Brandon's gorgeous back and butt cheeks were left to fend against the night air.

They moved to the hammock and piled several beach towels on top of them like a blanket. Without bothering to dress, they snuggled together for warmth and stared up at the stars. Cameron turned toward the shore and listened to the surf cascade onto the sand. He still couldn't comprehend that he had just jumped off a pier into the dark ocean, and he wondered what made him do it. Was it the challenge that this gorgeous, defiant man next to him presented? Or the sudden need to break free and live without fear of consequences? Whichever the reason, Cameron was sure that he would never have done it if it weren't for Brandon. Warm lips on his shoulder brought his attention back to the rock star lying at his side.

"So, what's it like to be an accountant in New York?"

"Dull." Cameron didn't have to think about the answer, especially after the party he just witnessed at the villa. "My mother wanted me to be a doctor, but I was a math geek. I enjoy finding tax loopholes." He smiled to himself and fought the urge to shake his head. God, he sounded like such a nerd. "I broke my poor mother's heart when I told her I didn't want to go to med school."

Brandon let out a short laugh. "Haven't we all? Can you imagine the look on my parents' faces when I told them I wasn't going to college and pursuing a career as a singer instead?"

Cameron smiled back. "I guess we both had our own agendas."

"Yeah. No one was telling me what to do when I was a teenager. I drove my parents crazy."

The image of a rebellious Brandon Bullet, causing havoc and running wild, made Cameron smile. Although Cameron's teen years were tame, he also had a stubborn streak and chose to follow his own reasoning, rather than that of his mother.

He turned back to the ocean as a light flashed in the blackness. It was a cruise ship passing along in the distance, and it dotted the horizon with tiny lights. "This is really beautiful." He sighed and rested his head on Brandon's shoulder. They lie together quietly, just listening to the sounds of the night, until a hard appendage jabbed Cameron in the thigh. He shifted his eyes from the sky to Brandon and was greeted with a lecherous grin. Those gorgeous blue eyes shone in the little bit of light that bled from the villas, and lit Cameron's heart on fire. This man stirred so many emotions inside of him. His entire world was turned upside down from the moment they met. It had been one of the best days of Cameron's life, but it wasn't over yet, and he wasn't letting this man go without having him one more time.

Cameron covered Brandon with his body, and their cocks pressed together like steel. He placed a deep kiss on Brandon's lips and drank in their luscious flavor. There was still a slight residue of salt from the ocean, and it spiced up the sweetness of Brandon's mouth. Cameron was so vested in tasting this man that he was unprepared when Brandon rolled over and reversed their positions. A small smile permeated the kiss. "Just because you're on top doesn't mean you win." Cameron knew that tussling on the unsteady hammock would end with them both in the sand, so he was content to let Brandon lie on top of him. Besides, he could easily control things from the bottom. He dug his hands into the hard slabs of Brandon's butt cheeks and thrust upwards. He gyrated his pelvis, so their cocks circled one another. It was an erotic rotation of muscle against muscle.

Brandon tried to counter the movement, but Cameron held his hips firmly in place, so he resorted to jutting his hips forward, while Cameron kept a steady grinding motion from underneath. Brandon buried his forehead into Cameron's shoulder and exhaled a deep shuddering breath. "Fuck," he whispered, and pressed down harder.

The hammock swayed underneath them, and the rough material scratched at Cameron's naked skin. Each movement sent a gritty rub of friction across his back and buttocks, accompanied by a ripple of pleasure at his groin. The contradiction of sensations – coarse and grainy in back, smooth and tingling in front – had Cameron burning up with passion.

Brandon suddenly rolled to the side so now they were facing one another. The hammock rocked, and the beach towels that had been acting like a blanket fell from their bodies, exposing their naked flesh to the salted air. It was a refreshing breeze on Cameron's overheated skin. They both grabbed each other's cock at the same time and let out a simultaneous grunt. Their techniques were similar – long, tight strokes that made certain to hit the most sensitive part at the tip.

The combination of the strong hand stroking him, the intoxicating scent of Brandon's long hair, still damp from the water, and the voracious kiss that robbed Cameron of oxygen, left him lightheaded. Brandon's fist pumped harder, and his tongue pressed deeper, arousing Cameron even more. Oh, God, he was ready to explode!

But it was Brandon who came first with a hard jolt of his hips. He broke the kiss and took in a deep breath of air, while warm ribbons of fluid shot from his body.

With his lover satiated, Cameron let go and allowed the pleasure to wash over him. Brandon's hand had tightened, and it brought an exquisite pressure that made a tremor run down Cameron's leg. His entire body tingled like a thousand hands were on him, then he came with a full-body shudder that shook the hammock.

Brandon's lips were on him again, this time gentler. It was a good thing, because Cameron was out of strength and unprepared for another tangle with this man who seemed to thrive on challenging him. He enjoyed the slower kiss immensely. Without the rough bout of posturing, he was free to revel in the powerful connection that they shared.

They cleaned up with the towels and dressed, then resumed their walk on the beach. Neither one said anything while they strolled with their bare feet in the surf and their arms around one another. They were content to be alone, sharing the night and the closeness of the other's body. Words seemed unimportant.

They walked in silence for a long time, and Cameron could feel the hours dwindling. It meant their time together would come to an end, and he would most likely never see Brandon again. It tore at Cameron's heart like a razor.

Their footsteps slowed and Cameron stopped to face Brandon. He cupped Brandon's face in his hands and kissed him. Their bodies fell against one another, and the heat that transpired between them made Cameron's body flush red hot. The light from a nearby tiki torch hit Brandon's blue eyes, and they burned into Cameron's heart. "Isn't it crazy that we just met today? I feel like we've known each other so much longer."

"Me too. I wish I wasn't leaving in a few hours. I want you to come to the show tomorrow night in Sao Paolo. We're leaving right afterward, but I'd really like to be able to look into the audience, or at the side of the stage, and see your face." Brandon gave Cameron another soft kiss and brushed his hand against Cameron's cheek. "I'll be tied up all day with sound check and promo stuff, but I could send a car for you."

It warmed Cameron's heart to know that Brandon had the same strong feelings, which only seemed to escalate as dawn drew nearer. Although he would much rather spend tomorrow night alone with Brandon, the idea of watching Brandon and his band play a full-length concert was an unexpected bonus. "I'd really like that, Brandon. I want to spend more time with you, and I'd love to see you perform on stage."

CHAPTER THREE

Cameron had never been to a rock concert in his life, but he was as eager as a teenage groupie. Driving to the arena in the back of a chauffeured stretch limousine only enhanced the experience and fed his excitement. The ride seemed to take forever, but at last the venue was within sight. Cameron leaned toward the window to get a closer look. Concertgoers littered the block and security was everywhere. A large group of fans raced toward the car as it pulled up to the back entrance of the arena. Security guards manned the barricades to keep them safely at bay, but they rallied against it.

Cameron exited the limo, and the exuberance of the crowd deflated when they saw that he wasn't one of their favorite rock stars, but some continued to gawk at him, intrigued by his identity and arrival in the expensive car. He gave his name to a burly guard who ceremoniously stepped aside and granted him admission. Cameron followed a long corridor filled with activity. People passed him in both directions, too busy to answer his questions about where to find Brandon. He continued through the hallway and checked each door until he came upon one with Brandon's name on it. Cameron's heart fluttered as he stared at the little black and white card in the metal holder on the door, and he knocked with impatience. A rush of loud music and voices spilled from the room when a security guard answered.

"Name?" The guard blocked his path.

"I'm Cameron Douglas. Brandon is expecting me."

The security guard checked a clipboard, then stepped aside so Cameron could enter. The room was thick with people, and Cameron navigated through them in search of his star. The sweet smell of pot infiltrated Cameron's senses. Someone seated on the couch was snorting coke off a magazine. Two guys were groping each other against the wall next to a buffet table filled with an enormous spread of food. A bartender poured drinks behind a full bar located to Cameron's right. This impressive pre-show party could easily pass for the main event.

A pair of hands, covered in fingerless gloves, circled Cameron's waist from behind and startled him. Lips tickled his neck, and then Brandon's voice was in his ear.

"I thought you'd never get here."

Cameron turned to face his lover, expecting the sandy-haired boyish face from the night before. His mouth dropped open when he was greeted by a rock and roll god. Brandon's day-old razor stubble had grown in scruffy and toughened his jaw. His intense blue eyes were rimmed in dark black eyeliner. Tight, ripped jeans hugged his body, while his bare chest displayed his black and grey tattoos and the silver barbells that pierced his nipples. His soft curls were tousled with a just-rolled-out-of-bed look that made Cameron's heart, and his erection, rush with adrenaline. Gone was the guise of an ordinary man. In its wake stood Brandon Bullet, Rock Star.

Brandon let out a small chuckle. "I know I look a little different from yesterday. It's kind of fun to dress like the average guy, but it's just a disguise. This is the way I normally dress. This is the real me. Everyone knows I'm flashy, so when I shave my face clean, tie my hair back and wear regular clothes, no one recognizes me. I can easily go undercover by downplaying my appearance." His smile deflated a little, and worry lines settled on his forehead. "Do you like it? Is it too much?"

"I fucking love it." The Brandon Bullet of last night was anything but ordinary. He was sexy and handsome. The Brandon Bullet that was in front of Cameron today was a steaming, scorching hot, sexy mountain of molten heat. The packaging differed greatly, but the same sweet person resided beneath. He grabbed Brandon by the chin, covered his mouth in a smoldering kiss, and ran his fingers through Brandon's gorgeous head of disheveled hair. Their cocks bumped into each other like two massive bundles of stone.

"Let's go somewhere a little quieter," Brandon said. "I'm sorry there are so many people here. They just show up since I have the biggest dressing room."

Brandon led Cameron down the hall to another dressing room which had Derek's name on the door, and they slipped inside. It was substantially smaller than Brandon's dressing room, but it still had an elaborate display of food and a fully stocked bar. Brandon pulled Cameron onto the plump leather sofa and caught him in a potent kiss.

It might be Cameron's imagination, but Brandon seemed more dominant in his rock and roll attire. But Cameron wasn't about to back down just because Brandon's appearance was more aggressive and intimidating. He took control of the kiss and wrapped his arms around Brandon's upper body.

"Are we going to play this game again?" Brandon asked with a mischievous sparkle in his flaming blue eyes.

"Afraid you'll lose again, rock star?"

"Not at all. I let you win last night."

Cameron threw his head back and laughed. "Sure, you did."

Brandon chuckled and shook his head, then kissed him again. "How was the ride from Rio?"

Cameron hadn't been prepared for the five-hour drive. He had been anxious and impatient, but the inside of the luxurious car had offered him a small distraction in the way of a flat-panel television. "I felt like a celebrity. Thanks for sending a limo, but it really wasn't necessary."

"I wasn't going to let you take the bus." Brandon displayed a teasing smile. "I know it was a long ride. I wanted you to be comfortable. You must be hungry. Let's eat." He went to the buffet and loaded two plates with food. After he set them down on the coffee table, he retrieved a bottle of champagne and two glasses and returned to the seat next to Cameron. "I wish we had some candles."

57

The romantic, intimate meal contrasted with Brandon's hard rocker exterior and melted Cameron's heart. "Did you set this up?"

Brandon nodded with modesty. "I wanted to make our last meal together special, and I knew we wouldn't have any privacy in my dressing room."

"Thank you. This is really nice." Cameron placed his hand on Brandon's thigh as a gesture of appreciation, but it quickly turned erotic, and they both stared down at it.

Brandon leaned close enough so his breath tickled Cameron's lips in the barest of a kiss. It was soft, gentle and weightless. "Let's eat first." He skewered one of the thin slices of steak with his fork and slid it around in the tangy sauce. Instead of bringing it to his mouth, he offered it to Cameron.

A tiny drop of the precious liquid threatened to fall from the end of the meat. Cameron quickly extended his tongue and caught it before it dripped onto his knee. Brandon placed the morsel on Cameron's tongue, and his mouth closed around it. The tender beef melted in his mouth. It was succulent and juicy, and moisture spurted from within as his teeth sank into it.

Next, Brandon skewered a carrot and held it inches from Cameron's lips.

"For me?" Cameron asked with a coy smile.

Brandon nodded and touched the vegetable to Cameron's mouth. He glided the soft edge of the carrot across Cameron's bottom lip, where it left a covering of sweet glaze. Brandon licked it off. "You taste delicious."

Every fiber in Cameron's body was tingling. Food had never been such a delicate seduction. Brandon taunted him with the carrot and dangled it just out of reach. He grabbed Brandon's hand with impatience and sucked down the robust, sweet vegetable.

Brandon pierced several carrots and a big piece of beef onto the end of the fork for himself. He held Cameron's gaze while he slowly chewed.

Cameron watched Brandon's lips churning. Images of those lips on his body last night filled his thoughts with an erotic show that was hard to dismiss, until a tiny round potato was offered to him. The soft rose-colored skin was dimpled and speckled, and he wanted it in his mouth. It was firm on his tongue until he bit into it, and then the warm center exploded with a warm, buttery flavor.

Brandon took another red potato and slowly sucked it from the fork with his luscious lips. He purposefully rolled it around his mouth for several seconds before he crushed it between his teeth. He popped another potato in his mouth. Then he slid his hand around the back of Cameron's neck, and their lips met in a kiss.

Cameron expected a visit from a thick, tasty tongue, but got a tiny round potato instead. He gobbled it up with greed. "I want some meat," Cameron demanded with a breathy voice.

Brandon dug his fork into a thick slice of beef. He soaked up some of the juice on the plate, then skewered a chunk of carrot on the end. The forkful of food filled Cameron's mouth and satiated its emptiness with zest.

Brandon smiled as he watched Cameron devour the food. "Is that too much? Is it too big?"

Cameron shook his head and swallowed. "My throat is endless. It can tolerate a lot bigger." The teasing smile slid off Brandon's face, and his eyes glazed over. The lustful expression was an arousing sight that made Cameron's cock ache. He picked up a glass of champagne and drank, then tipped it to Brandon's lips so he could partake of the effervescent liquid.

Brandon stabbed several pieces of the delectable meat with his fork and stuffed it in Cam's mouth. Cameron chewed it with an insatiable desire while Brandon watched with yearning.

Cameron picked up the fork and offered Brandon several slices of beef. Brandon held Cameron's wrist steady while he sucked the juicy meat into his mouth.

They took turns feeding each other, until Cameron fell back onto the couch, engorged and satisfied. He was done with dinner. He wanted to feast on the rock star seated next to him. He put his arms around the wonderful man and stared into his eyes. "That was an incredible meal. I'll never forget this dinner, Brandon. Thank you for making a memory that will last a lifetime."

Brandon answered with a slow, tender kiss that Cameron wished could last forever. He placed his hand on Brandon's cheek and infiltrated his mouth with his tongue. He tasted the juicy meat and tangy sauce, buttery potatoes, and sweet carrots. Delicious. His lips went to Brandon's neck and sucked at his flesh. His mouth traveled down the hard muscles of Brandon's chest, and he found a perky nipple. The metal barbell was hard against his teeth and cold against the heat of his mouth. Brandon's nipple tightened and became a rigid point around the metal piercing. The other nipple beckoned, and Cameron answered. He decided that this nipple needed more attention and sucked it mercilessly while Brandon rolled his head back and moaned.

Brandon's shoulders rose from the back of the couch, and he grabbed Cameron by the chin. "I'm taking the lead today." He pulled Cameron's shirt over his head and tossed it on the floor. He made Cameron sit back and then sank to his knees between Cameron's legs.

It happened so quickly that Cameron didn't have a chance to resist. The small act of submission kicked up his endorphins. It was a new role for him, and it made the blood pump through his veins.

Brandon covered Cameron's chest with soft nips and a rough swipe of his tongue. He ran his hands down the curve of Cameron's biceps and explored every inch of Cameron's torso with succulent kisses. He opened Cameron's belt buckle and the top button of his jeans. The involuntary urge to take control took over, and Cameron grabbed Brandon by the wrists. Their eyes met with hot defiance. Both waited for the other to look away, but neither conceded. Impatient for Brandon's mouth on his cock, Cameron pushed his jeans down, but never broke eye contact.

A smile spread across Brandon's lips, and his eyes dropped to Cameron's dick, which was only an inch from his chin. "I'm too horny to fight you, plus I can't resist when your cock is this close to my face." He grabbed Cameron's cock in a tight grasp and fisted it with quick strokes. Cameron grunted and moaned from the rough foreplay and thrust his hips upwards. Brandon's mouth came down without warning and sucked Cameron hard enough to make him shudder.

Cameron ran his fingers through Brandon's mess of long hair and held onto a blond chunk. He attempted to guide Brandon's head, but Brandon was in complete rebellion and moved against Cameron's hand. If Cameron pushed down, Brandon pulled up. Brandon had his own momentum, which was fast and hard. Quick and deep – real deep. Cameron stopped fighting and melted into the couch cushion. It was freeing to give up control and let someone else take over. It allowed him the pleasure of enjoying every sensation that coursed through his body.

Cameron sighed heavily. His body burned with a fiery tingle. He spread his legs and threw his head back. He panted loudly while his cock twitched every few seconds. Brandon sucked with such force that his cheeks were two hollow gullies, and the slurping noises coming from his mouth was a glorious sound.

Brandon's lips released their suction and attached themselves to Cameron's balls. Momentarily blindsided by a rush of surprised pain, Cameron flinched. But the quick jolt of pain turned into mild discomfort, and then into pleasure. Brandon's tongue danced over Cameron's sac and covered it with tiny love bites. He pulled off Cameron's sneakers and freed his legs from his jeans, all without removing his mouth from Cameron's crotch. He threw Cameron's legs over his shoulders. Cameron opened his thighs wider and slid down lower on the couch. Brandon's hot, wet tongue traveled between Cameron's butt cheeks and prodded his hole with hard flicks. Brandon's tongue was thick and commanding and moved in a frenzied swirl. Cameron never wanted it to leave his body. It was so different to lie still and helpless and let someone bestow unreciprocated pleasure.

His eyes suddenly flipped open. He stared down at Brandon between his legs, taking full control, and a defiant smile spread across his face. His assertive confidence kicked in. "You think you're in charge, don't you?"

Brandon smiled and nodded without removing his mouth from Cameron's cock.

Cameron grabbed Brandon by the upper arms, pulled him up and pinned him to the couch in one quick motion. Stunned by the sudden reversal of their positions, Brandon recoiled, and his mouth hung open. It was pouty and full, and his bottom lip glistened with saliva. Cameron sucked on it and then pushed his tongue inside to deliver a controlling kiss.

When Cameron pulled back, Brandon had a hypnotic haze covering his electric blue eyes.

"I can't believe what you do to me, Cam. You stir things inside of me that I never knew existed. The way you manhandle me is infuriating and intoxicating at the same time."

A deep breath left Cameron's lungs. He knew, firsthand, the rush of adrenaline that their power play ignited. "I want to fuck you. I want to be inside you. Let me show you how good I can make you feel."

Brandon's eyes grew a little wider, and he nodded his head ever so slightly.

Filled with overwhelming excitement, Cameron's heart pounded in his chest. His mouth came down on Brandon's with a hard kiss, but

Brandon wasn't ready to entirely relinquish control and held their mouths together with a firm hand on the back of Cameron's neck.

Cameron was so riled up that all he wanted to do was fuck Brandon until he cried out with ecstasy. He licked a trail down Brandon's chest and gave a hard bite to each dark, round nipple. He tugged on Brandon's belt and freed the clasp. The zipper of his jeans sliced open with a gritty screech and released his cock from the constraints of the denim. Cameron gave a short laugh when he saw that Brandon hadn't bothered to wear any underwear. "Presumptuous, were you?"

Brandon gave him a crooked smile. "Hopeful." He kicked off his boots and stripped himself of his jeans so that they were both naked.

Cameron remained stationed between Brandon's legs and stroked his cock. He toyed with the bulbous head. It offered a beautiful drop of fluid that coated the tip in silky lubrication. Brandon covered Cameron's hand and guided it up and down his cock, but Cameron pushed it away. "You're supposed to sit back and let me do the work."

"I can't relax." Brandon's breath was heavy. "I can't believe I'm going to let you fuck me." His eyes disappeared behind his lids for a moment. "Just saying the words out loud has me ready to come. Do it. I want you to fuck me, Cam."

Exhilarated by the mental picture and dirty talk, Cameron lunged forward and kissed Brandon. Their tongues twirled with passion and impatience. He broke the kiss when a condom was pressed into his hand. He looked down at the square packet, then up at Brandon, who had a sexy smile on his face while he dangled a small plastic tube of lubricating jelly.

With his mouth on Brandon's cock, Cameron's slicked fingers circled Brandon's hole until it was well coated. He pushed one finger inside, all the way to the third knuckle.

Brandon grunted, and he ran his hands down the length of his thighs. He placed his legs over Cameron's shoulders, one at a time, and dug the heels of his feet into Cameron's back.

Cameron plunged his finger deeper and watched the bliss that passed over Brandon's face. Brandon inhaled a deep breath and his eyelids flickered. He moistened his lower lip with a seductive brush of his tongue, and they both let out a long sigh at the same time.

Cameron's lips fell onto the hard abs that graced Brandon's belly. His nerve endings were jumping inside him, impatient to take this gorgeous man. He twisted his fingers and scissored them inside Brandon until he was stretched enough to comfortably accept Cameron's cock, which was growing more engorged with each second that passed.

Cameron rolled the condom onto his weeping cock and lathered Brandon's bottom with lube. He reminded himself to go slow as the tip of his cock breached Brandon's ass, even though he wanted to ram himself balls deep inside Brandon's hole. He slowly pumped his hips until his cock was fully buried. Brandon's muscles clenched and contracted with each thrust and milked Cameron's cock with delightful pressure.

Brandon was tight. He probably hadn't bottomed in a long time. Endorphins shot through Cameron like a rapid-fire machine gun. The rush of intimacy and surge of heat took him by surprise. His body tingled and the hairs on the back of his neck stood up. Each thrust of his hips brought him closer to euphoria.

Brandon moaned and rolled his head to the side. He adjusted his legs over Cameron's shoulders to afford a better angle, but he didn't need a better angle. Every movement was better than the last and escalated the mounting pleasures inside Cameron's body. He took Brandon's cock in his hand and started pumping it to the same rhythm of his hips. On the edge of a titillating orgasm, Cameron thrust himself harder and faster. His hand tugged on Brandon's cock and succumbed to a throbbing bolt of lightning and shot his load inside Brandon's bottom. He opened his eyes just in time to see white, hot liquid spurt from Brandon's cock all over his magnificent abs. One final thrust of his hips and Cameron let out a long moan before he fell on top of Brandon with exhaustion.

"Holy shit." Brandon squeezed Cameron in a hug and panted in his ear.

Cameron couldn't respond. He was too overwhelmed by the emotions that ran through his body. They lay together on the couch with their bodies entwined for several minutes, before Cameron disposed of the used condom into a napkin on the coffee table. When he turned back, Brandon had a humble softness to his eyes and small intimate smile on his lips.

"That was really nice. I haven't bottomed in years." He brushed his fingers across Cameron's cheek. "I'm glad it was with you. It's a lot of pressure being the frontman in a famous band. It was nice to take a step back and out of the driver's seat for once. I couldn't do that with just anyone, though. It needed to be with someone I trusted."

There was that vulnerability again, and Cameron's heart melted into a pool of liquid. "I'm glad it was with me too." Cameron cupped Brandon's face in his hands and stared into his eyes. He would give anything to stay with Brandon for a few more days, and the center of his chest was suddenly pounding with a dull ache.

Brandon traced a finger across the profile of Cameron's cheek. "Why do you look sad?"

Understanding passed between them, and heartache surrounded them.

"Is there any chance you can come on tour with us?" Brandon asked.

"I wish I could, but I have to be back at work Monday morning. This was just a quick trip to break my bad mood and stop me from feeling sorry for myself."

"Did it?"

"This has been the best weekend of my life, Brandon. I had no idea we'd connect on such a deep level. Are we going to keep in touch?"

"I want to, Cam. I really want to see you again."

"Me too." It was the truth, but reality stood in the way. Cameron was chained to his New York City office, and Brandon was a rock star who toured the world. He could never keep up with Brandon's hectic schedule, and long-distance relationships never lasted. "When do you get back home to L.A.?"

"I think there's another three months left to the tour. I don't remember where we're headed half the time. Promo parties. Meet and greets. Shows. Television appearances. Our manager or PR rep usually just tells us where to go."

"You sound exhausted just talking about it. Do you ever slow down?"

Brandon shook his head. "I can't. We gotta ride this roller coaster while it's in motion, because it could stop at any minute. I've worked my entire life for this. It's everything I've ever wanted, but it does get tiring. And lonely."

Someone pounded on the door and startled both of them. "Put it in your pants, Brandon! We're on in ten. Felix is about to shit his pants because you're not in your dressing room."

An unexpected laugh bubbled from Cameron's throat, and it lightened the somber mood. "Who's shitting his pants?"

"That would be our manager. To be fair, we're not exactly known for our punctuality." His bandmate banged on the door again, and Brandon rolled his eyes. "I'm coming!"

"Yeah. I'll bet you are."

There was snickering behind the door, and Brandon and Cameron shared an affectionate smile and a small laugh.

They cleaned themselves up as quickly as they could and dressed. Brandon checked his hair in the mirror. It was untamed and disheveled. He smiled at Cameron. "You should fix my hair before every show." He laced his fingers through Cameron's hand, and they headed for the door.

"I hope you like loud music, because you've got the best seat in the house."

The stage lights swirled in flashes of red, blue and purple, and the smoke machine created an opaque cloudy haze that blanketed the stage. Alan sat straight ahead, pounding out beats on his drums loud enough to wake the dead. Jeremy and Derek, the bass player and the guitarist, were back to back dueling with their instruments. The twang of the guitar wailed into the arena, then the low grungy notes of the bass bellowed back with defiance. The crowd cheered and screamed and stomped their feet.

Someone threw a jock strap on stage. Derek picked it up and sniffed it, which caused a ripple of laughter through the arena. He clutched it to his chest, then placed the undergarment on his mic stand for safekeeping.

Cameron's gaze moved to the front of the stage and settled on Brandon. Encapsulated in a triangle of white light, Brandon stretched one arm out toward the crowd. Fans surged forward and tried to grasp his hand, all enamored by the charismatic lead singer.

Brandon soaked up the attention of the crowd. He leaped down into the space between the stage and the barricade, and the fans let loose with an explosive roar. They lunged toward him in an attempt to touch any part of his body they could get their hands on. A fan latched onto his arm and tugged him against the railing. Cameron's heart momentarily caught in his throat until security stepped in and dislodged the overzealous fan.

Brandon jumped back on stage but teetered on the apron. With the mic at his lips, he shook his long hair at the crowd. It glowed under the lights in soft waves of spun gold. He screamed the lyrics into the mic with a raunchy snarl, and the crowd hollered back with their fists in the air. There were 20,000 people in the audience, and they were all focused on Brandon.

The enormity of Brandon's fame hit Cameron like a brick to the face. His lover was a rock star! Cameron's chest puffed out with pride. There was a room full of cheering fans, all rushing at the stage to be closer to Brandon and his band. Their energy was contagious. The blaring music had Cameron's heart pounding against his ribcage, and there was a rush of blood flowing through his veins. He tapped his foot and bobbed his head to the beat of the drum. He was having the time of his life!

Brandon's hair flew around his face in a wild mass of curls, and his bare chest glistened with a thin film of perspiration that covered his tattoos with a soft sheen. In the middle of the revelry, he spun around and made eye contact with Cameron, still screaming into the mic with heart-stopping lyrics. The moment their eyes met, excitement exploded in Cameron's chest, and he raised his fist in the air, mimicking the salute of the fans.

Cameron scanned the stage full of handsome rock stars. Alan was the only one with short hair. He hammered his boots into the pedals of twin bass drums, and his arms were a blur of tattooed muscle. Jeremy stood on one of the amps with his bass slung low across his hips. His dark hair bounced off his tatted shoulders as he plucked the strings of his bass with a seductive thrust of his pelvis that accentuated each note. Derek was on his knees at the front of the stage, hunched over his guitar with his long hair cascading over his face like a veil of black mink. And then there was Brandon. He was at the center mic with his arms stretched wide open. The curve of his shoulders and biceps were like two small boulders that reflected the lights. The contoured muscles in his naked back flexed under the physical exertion of projecting his voice through the arena. His skin-tight jeans outlined Brandon's totally bitable ass.

The fans were wild and unruly. Crowd surfers floated over the audience and were dropped onto the arena floor. Fans sang along to the incoherent lyrics and rocked their heads to the heavy beat of the music.

Cameron watched the show with wide-eyed exuberance. Each song was exhilarating, and he never wanted the night to end. Pyrotechnics lit up the back of the stage. The fans screamed and waved rock and roll horns high above their heads. Brightly colored confetti blew through the arena. Then Brandon shouted the dreaded words, "Good night, Sao Paolo!" and Cameron's heart hit the floor. The 90-minute set flew by, and the end of the show meant that Brandon would be leaving in less than an hour, and Cameron may never see him again.

Although Cameron was enamored by Brandon Bullet, the rock star, it was Brandon Bullet, the man, who stole Cameron's heart. It was a weekend he would never forget, and he silently prayed that they wouldn't lose touch with one another.

Brandon exited the stage with his spirits as high as the moon. He threw his arms around Cameron in a powerful hug that lifted him off the floor. "I'm not used to someone waiting in the wings for me. It was exhilarating seeing you at the side of the stage when I was in the middle of a set."

"That was a fantastic show! You were awesome!" Happy laughter made its way into Cameron's throat and pushed out the melancholy knot. "I've never experienced anything like it! That was incredible! When are you playing the Tri-State area?"

"We played the East Coast at the beginning of the tour, but I'm sure we'll return . . . eventually."

Eventually. That goddamn knot in Cameron's throat returned, and it was the size of a fucking baseball.

Thirty minutes later, Cameron stood in front of the tour bus wrapped in Brandon's tight embrace. They held onto one another without a sliver of space between them. There were no words or heartfelt goodbyes, just an exchange of silent sentiment and a connection that took them both by surprise.

Brandon Bullet was the man who had pulled Cameron out of his funk. Not only did Brandon remind Cameron there was a world out there that was passing him by while he sulked in his apartment, but Brandon showed him that love was out there waiting for him as well. He wasn't going to find it sitting on his living room couch.

One weekend in paradise had changed Cameron more than he thought possible. He was happier than he had been in a long time, and yet, his heart was quickly dying. This was probably the last time he would lay eyes on Brandon Bullet. The lump in Cameron's throat threatened to cut off his air, and the sharp pain in his heart made a tear well in the corner of his eye. He had no idea it would be so hard to say goodbye.

A loud horn blared through the silent air to remind Brandon that everyone was waiting for him, and the engine of the massive tour bus came to life with a rumble.

Brandon pulled back far enough to look Cameron in the eyes but kept his hands on Cameron's shoulders. His voice was low and filled with emotion. "I gotta go. I'm sorry."

Cameron's voice wasn't much steadier. "I know."

"I'm going to miss you."

"I'm gonna miss you too."

"I'll call you tomorrow, and I'll text you the tour schedule as soon as I get it from my manager."

Cameron manipulated his mouth into a small smile, even though his heart was breaking. "Good. Because I want to see you perform again." Really, he just wanted to see Brandon again.

Brandon took Cameron's face in his hands and placed a long, delicate kiss on his lips. The kiss lingered while their tongues said a heart-wrenching goodbye. Cameron's body ached with sadness, and he reveled in their last kiss.

Their lips slowly parted.

"I'll see you around, Cameron Douglas."

"I'll see you soon, rock star."

Brandon took Cameron's hand and placed a gentle parting kiss on his knuckles. He walked backwards with slow steps, never averting his eyes or letting go of Cameron's hand. Their arms connected the space between them like a rope slowly fraying until distance broke the tie, and their fingers slowly drifted apart. The doors to the tour bus opened with a whoosh, and Brandon stepped inside. One last mournful look over his shoulder met Cameron's watery gaze, before the doors shut like an iron curtain. Bulletproof's tour bus rolled away and took a big chunk of Cameron's heart with it.

Jenna Galicki

CHAPTER FOUR

Three months later

Brandon tried Cam's cell phone number for the millionth time. He could barely hear the phone ringing on the other end over the boisterous crowd in his dressing room. Then the familiar series of high-pitched ringtones cut through the noise, followed by, "We're sorry, the number you have reached is no longer in service."

He threw the phone on the couch with more aggression than anticipated, and it bounced to the floor.

Derek handed it back to him. "What the fuck's wrong with you? Since we left Brazil, you've been a total bitch. We just played the last show of a kick-ass tour. We're at the LA Forum. We're home. Stop fucking sulking and move on."

He knew Derek was right, but the sting of rejection still burned Brandon's heart. He had exchanged a couple of text messages and calls with Cam the first few days after he left Sao Paolo, but then the connection went dead. Cam must have changed his number shortly after he had flown back home. Maybe the asshole ex-boyfriend was back.

Brandon had often thought about the bond he shared with Cam. At first it consoled him, but as the weeks turned into months without any contact from Cam, the memory only left him with a hole in his heart. It was an ache filled with unanswered questions. Now that the tour was over, he would return home, and the empty house would remind him that he was alone. He sighed and tried to let go of the lingering regret. There was nothing he could do if Cam had picked up with his life. He just hoped that Cam was happy, even if he was miserable without Cam.

Derek knocked Brandon's boot off of his knee. "Get the fuck up, and let's get a drink. You've got a bar full of alcohol and a room full of dudes, all ready to make you forget about any guy that's got you down."

Brandon wasn't interested, but alcohol would do nicely to fill the void and numb in regret in his heart.

Brandon slammed back a shot of Jack Daniels and was in the middle of pouring another one when a security guard shoved a bouquet of hot pink bromeliads at him. "Some guy has been hounding the bouncer at the side-stage entrance. He wouldn't leave until we promised to hand you these."

Memories of Rio de Janeiro and the path to the villas that was filled with greenery and bromeliads made Brandon's heart race. Could it really be Cam after all this time, without so much as a phone call to announce his arrival? He looked for a card but there was none. "What did the guy look like? What was his name?"

The security guard shrugged. "I'm just passing along the message."

Brandon ran from the dressing room, down the long corridor that led to the arena, and stopped in front of the heavy door. He flung it open, but the back of a muscle-bound security guard stood in his way and blocked his field of vision.

The guard turned around in surprise and opened a sightline into the venue.

"Brandon!"

It was Cam, waving like a lunatic, secured behind a barricade a few feet in front of the security guard. Joy filled Brandon's heart, and he couldn't have smiled any wider. "Let him through," he told the guard.

Cam bolted into Brandon's arms and hugged him so tight that it pushed the breath from his lungs. Brandon returned the tight embrace and clung to Cam. "I thought I'd never see you again." His elation suddenly turned emotional, and his voice cracked. "I've been trying to call you for two months."

"I know. I'm sorry." Cam grabbed Brandon's face in his hands and placed a powerful kiss on his mouth.

The familiar dominant and heavy-handed kiss set Brandon's heart on fire, and his cock immediately hardened. He wanted to ravage Cam's body right there in the corridor. He broke the kiss, defying his raging hormones. "What happened? Why did you change your number?"

Jenna Galicki

Cam's shoulders slumped, and he sighed. "My life kinda fell apart. I misplaced my phone. I never backed up my contacts on that stupid cloud thing, so when I got a new phone, everything was gone. Then I got laid off. When I lost my job, they took the phone back, and I had to get a new number. I had no way to get in touch with you. I was losing my fucking mind." Despair infiltrated Cam's face, and he slowly shook his head. "You were gone."

"I thought you didn't want to talk to me anymore. I was kind of heartbroken. I even thought about hiring a private detective to find you, but I thought you must have met someone." He never gave up trying Cam's phone number, though, on the off chance that the call would go through and Cam would answer. Even if Cam had moved on, at least there would have been some closure. He couldn't believe Cam was really standing in front of him now, and he looked just as distraught as Brandon had about losing touch with one another. "You flew all the way out here to L.A. on the chance that you'd get backstage to see me?"

Cam's enthusiastic smile could have lit up the arena. "I got a job on South Figueroa. I moved to L.A. a week ago."

Brandon thought he was dreaming. It was surreal that after months of no contact, Cam was here, in L.A., permanently.

Cam's smile wavered slightly, and concern clouded his eyes. "I know this is a surprise, and you weren't expecting me to move here. I don't know if your situation has changed. If you met someone or if you're not looking—"

A kiss cut off Cam's sentence. "You have no idea how happy I am right now, Cam. I want to get to know you better. I want a chance at a relationship with you. I missed you so much and couldn't get you out of my head. I want this more than anything. I want you."

A tear glistened in Cam's eye. "I'm really glad. I was worried about taking the job out here. I was afraid it was too bold of a move, but I had to take the chance. I haven't been able to stop thinking about you, either. I want to explore the possibility of a future with you, Brandon."

Brandon's heart beat a steady, happy rhythm. "I have no idea if you can handle my crazy life, Cam, but I'm going to do everything I can to make sure I don't make the same mistakes I've made in the past. I'll fly you out on weekends when I'm on tour, or I'll fly back between shows. I'll do whatever I have to do. I really want to pursue this and see if we can make it work."

"We're going to get that chance, Brandon, and it's going to start right now."

The End . . . For Now

Find out what happens next in Branded, Bulletproof Book 2

Jenna Galicki

Branded, Bulletproof Book 2

These two alpha males met with the force of a head-on collision. Sirens went off and lit up their hearts faster than a flash fire. But now that they're living in the real world, everything isn't as easy as anticipated. Other than their strong-willed and dominant personalities, they couldn't be more opposite.

As the frontman for a world-famous heavy metal band, Brandon Bullet lives in the spotlight. He thrives on the attention of his fans and the wild parties that all rock stars are accustomed to.

The free-spirited attitude and uninhibited lifestyle that is so natural to Brandon totally contradicts with Cameron Douglas' anal-retentive and structured mindset. Spurred on by a thirst for adventure, Cameron is ready to leave behind his sedate, low-key life, but he's unprepared for the rock star's world of free sex, drugs, and non-stop parties.

Concessions aren't always easy when thrust into a new relationship, especially with two headstrong men who constantly challenge one another. Add time apart from Bulletproof's promotional tour, and it's another layer of adjustment to contend with that just may push this newly united couple too far.

Sample: Branded, Bulletproof Book 2

"We only have a small window before fashionably-late turns into missing the event altogether."

Cam's head slowly lolled to the side, and he kissed Brandon's shoulder. "If it's all the same to you, I'd rather stay home and spend some time alone together. I've been working late. You've been rehearsing. We haven't spent much time together this week."

Brandon didn't care about the Tony's, but he never thought Cam would want to pass on the event. "Really? They're honoring Florence Henderson."

Cam perked up. "Mrs. Brady?"

"Yeah." Brandon chuckled.

"Meh." Cam shrugged. "On the other hand, if it was Peter Brady, I'd be dressed and out the door already."

Brandon let out a hearty laugh. "Greg was my favorite. Something about his hair always held my eye."

"It figures." Cam stretched like a lazy cat and snuggled into the couch cushion with his head resting on Brandon's shoulder.

"You're really not interested in going tonight?"

"It sounds like a lot of fun, but given the choice between them and you, I'd pick you every time." Cam placed his hand on Brandon's thigh. "They don't mean anything to me. You do."

Brandon stared at Cam, genuinely stunned. Anyone else would have jumped at the chance to attend a party where they could have one-on-one casual conversations with a room full of A-listers. Cam couldn't care less. He was constantly reinforcing the notion that fame and notoriety meant nothing to him. Past experiences with so many guys who were just looking to add a name to their list of rock-star conquests, or a quick ticket to fame, made it hard for Brandon to remember that Cam wasn't like any of them. Cam was as genuine and honest as any man could be. He was sincere and modest. It was such a refreshing change to be able to trust someone without questioning and second guessing the intention behind every compliment and every action. There were no ulterior motives. There was no game plan. Cam was just Cameron Douglas, a guy who cared about Brandon Bullet for the man he was, faults and all.

"Are you disappointed?" Cam asked when Brandon was silent.

"You never disappoint me, Cam. You constantly reinforce your integrity. It's hard for me to trust people. Everybody wants something. But not you. I knew you were different right away. I trust you with my heart, and I can't remember the last time that's happened." A lump cut off Brandon's sentence. Finding Cam was literally a dream come true. Finding him twice was a miracle, and he didn't want to risk losing him ever again.

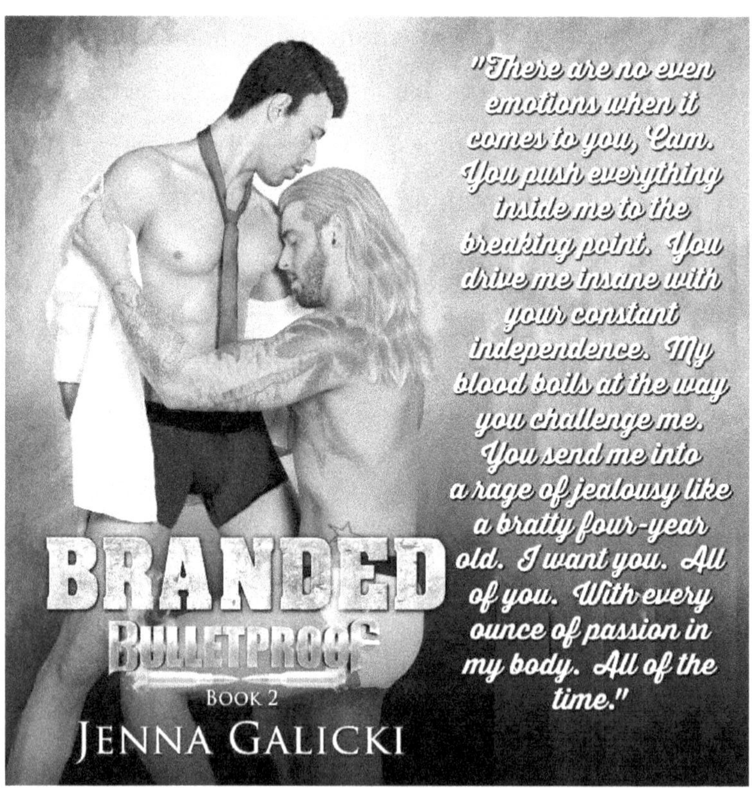

Other Books in the Bulletproof Series:

Bassist With Benefits, Bulletproof Book 3 – Jeremy and Alan's story - a friends-to-lovers rock star romance.

Bandmates and best friends since they were teens, Jeremy Kagan and Alan Delgado share everything – including men. But their brotherly bond was shattered during one incident of mistaken identity in a darkened bedroom when a line was crossed. With boundaries broken and the line of friendship blurred, they struggle to move forward.

For Jeremy, that night was a dream come true. He had been in love with Alan for a decade but had been too afraid to bare his heart and reveal his true feelings. Now that the opportunity has presented itself, he's ready to seize the moment. This is his one chance to be with the only man he's ever loved.

Alan, on the other hand, isn't dealing with the incident so well. A lot of monumental achievements have occurred in his life, but none were as life altering as a single erotic encounter with his best friend. The usual fun-loving camaraderie he and Jeremy had always shared is now awkward and uncomfortable.

Unable to shed the memory of their rendezvous, Alan starts to look at Jeremy in a new light. Transitioning from bromance to romance isn't as easy as expected, especially since Alan isn't ready to share their newfound bond with anyone else. Stress from keeping their relationship a secret turns explosive as these two battle their passion in private. Now they need to figure out if it's worth risking everything, including their friendship, in order to pursue a future together as a couple.

Jenna Galicki

BULLETPROOF, Bulletproof Book 4 – Derek's story.

Two wild, out-of-control rock stars. One at the top of his career living the high life and enamored by the glitz and the glam. The other, just starting out and too sensitive for the rough-and-tumble world of a rock star.

Derek MacAlister, the wild one. Known for dancing on tabletops, partying too hard and possessing a never-ending thirst for excitement. With his bandmates now settled in committed relationships, he's the last man standing. The only problem is that he wants to party all night long, but his best friends are content to stay at home. Enter Travis Fontana, a bad boy with a reputation for trouble, and Derek has his partner in crime.

Travis Fontana just scored the gig of a lifetime opening for the nation's top heavy metal band. He's a rebel who thrives on pushing the limits of a good time and Bulletproof's sexy long-haired guitarist, Derek MacAlister, is right by his side to share the fun. Together, they're double trouble.

But all is not as it seems. Underneath the painted-on smile and carefree exterior that Travis shows the world lies a tortured soul with a dark past. Little by little, Travis lets Derek see a side of him that no one else knows. Derek, unused to the unfiltered raw honesty that Travis shares, finds that he wants to take care of this troubled, vulnerable man and turns out to be Travis' rock in times of crisis.

When the pressures of new-found fame begin to overwhelm Travis, he quickly starts to unravel. Pushed to the breaking point, it becomes clear that even Derek can't save him. Travis needs to save himself.

Jenna Galicki

"I'm so sorry about everything I put you through. I never wanted to expose you to any of it."

"I wanted to help you. Didn't you know that?"

BULLETPROOF
Bulletproof Book 4

Follow up with the Holiday Collection:

A Bulletproof Christmas
Three sexy stories. One epic wedding.

A Bulletproof New Year
Three Tantalizing Tales. Two sweet. One salty.

Praise for the Bulletproof Series:

"The fight for dominance was freaking HELLA HOT! I need more Cam and Brandon in my world! " - *Amazon Reader*

"I was so utterly amazed at the depth of this story and the heartfelt emotions that I had while reading it. I was entranced and I couldn't stop reading. . .you feel [Derek and Travis'] pain and sadness, their joy and happiness and that is absolutely beautiful writing." - Amazon Reader

"There was an incredible rush and energy in Jeremy and Alan's story that was mesmorising and hooked me in completely. The chemistry between them was off the charts both on and off the stage. Well worth the read." - LMB Book Blog

"This series is everything. The music, the men, the band, the friendship, the love, it is all amazing and perfect." - Amazon Reader

The **BULLETPROOF** Series

The Holiday Collection

Other Books by Jenna Galicki

Street of Dreams

One street touched a thousand lives and sent two boys in opposite directions.

For Reid Mackenzie, Street of Dreams offers hope for a better life and a chance to share his music with the world. For Jake King, it reinforces his life of crime and the ties to a city that empowers him.

They were two boys, growing up side by side in the same neighborhood, but their lives couldn't be more different. Mac comes from a humble Scottish family and dreams of the stage and the day he has enough money to escape Chicago's South Side. Jake knows he'll never leave. The impoverished city, and his notorious father, have a hold on him that won't let go.

Circumstances force them to carry on their relationship in private, until it explodes in the worst way. With the will of a warrior, Jake vows he'll do whatever he has to in order for them to be together, no matter how brutal the consequences.

This is a story of courage, kilts, and second chances.

Praise for Street of Dreams:

★★★★★ Street of Dreams is riveting, exceptional and all-consuming. I am still shocked by how amazing this Jenna Galicki book is. It is definitely one hell of an impressive read.

★★★★★ A high angst roller coaster that you will not want to put down...This is one that will be read more than once.

★★★★★ I hurt for both of them. Basically, I was as wrecked as they both were.... if you're in the mood to be agonizingly destroyed, read on.

★★★★★ I loved how multi - dimensional each personality was in this story...The relationship between Jake and Mac was boiling hot, but it's development on the pages left me with a mouth hanging open.

★★★★★ I loved the banter/ hate love/ torment that the characters had going on. Omg it was crazy chemistry and I loved every page of it.

Radical Rock Stars Series:

The Prince of Punk Rock, Book 1 (Finalist 2015 Bisexual Book Awards. Winner, Angel, Tommy & Jessi, Saints & Sinners Couples Battle. Winner, Jessi Blade, Best Rocker Babe)
I love her, but I also love him.
She's everything to me.
He sets my world on fire.
It's our dirty little secret, and it's about to blow our record deal sky high.
I'm Tommy Blade, the Prince of Punk Rock, and this is our story.

Between A Rock and A Hard Place, Book 2
She's a rock goddess.
He's a sex pistol.
I need them both, in my life and in my bed, and I'm not living without either one of them.
I'll do whatever it takes, even if it costs me everything I've ever wanted.
I'm Tommy Blade, The Prince of Punk Rock, and this is the continuation of our story.

Punk Rock Resurrection, Book 3
This is a dark tale of loneliness and self-worth, and how the love of a woman can change a man.
My world was dark and filled with pain.
Loneliness gnawed at my soul.
I found solace in a bottle.
Music was my only refuge . . . until I met her.
She was a dark Gothic goddess in thigh-high leather boots.
She brought light into my life and showed me what it was like to be loved.
But could she handle the demons that haunted me . . . and the vices that kept them at bay?

Rock Star Redemption, Book 4
I live life in the fast lane.
My days and nights are a never-ending party of women, fast cars and alcohol.
I'm the one your daddy warned you about.
I have everything I ever wanted—except Audra Abelman.
She was always the good girl.
She was off limits.
I held out for almost a decade.
It's time to set her inner bad girl free.
I'm Jimmy Wilder, and I'm going to claim the most sought-after girl in the record industry.

Punk Rock-A-Bye Baby, Book 5
Revisit our original trio and follow up with the evolution of Angel, Tommy & Jessi's relationship. Time only makes this trio burn hotter!
She rocks my world.
He sets my soul on fire.
We've traveled down a bumpy road, but we've finally found the balance.
It's time to bring a new little rock star into our lives.
I'm Tommy Blade, the Prince of Punk Rock, and this is the next chapter in our story.

The Stage, Book 6 (an Immortal Angel/Bulletproof crossover novella)
Even rock stars get starstruck. Meeting heavy metal icon Brandon Bullet is a dream come true for Tommy Blade. When Immortal Angel decides to add Tommy's rock star idol as a guest singer to their set at the Get Rocked Festival, sparks fly and egos collide.

Epilogue by Brandon Bullet of Bulletproof.

The Roadie, Book 7 (an Immortal Angel/Bulletproof crossover novel)
"Let's live the dream. Let's make the fairy tale come true."

This isn't an angsty, tear-your-heart-out, ugly-cry romance. This is a love story.

Thirty days on tour with a sexy, bearded and tattooed roadie is exactly what Kira Abelman needs in order to light up her boring life with passion. It's supposed to be a no-strings-attached good time, but it turns into so much more. She knew their time together had an expiration date, but she isn't ready to say goodbye. Can Kira finally get her happily ever after and prove that fairy tales do come true?

Punk Rock Reflection, Book 8
Tommy Blade has it all—a hot wife, a sexy husband, and mega-stardom. His band is at the top of the charts, and his talent on the guitar has earned him worldwide recognition as an icon in the industry. Although the road to the top wasn't easy, his life has been one great achievement after another. But it leaves him wondering where to go from here.

Unable to find a future goal that excites him, he's stuck. A drastic change is just what he needs to shake up his life, because sometimes you have to lose everything in order to find what really matters.

Punk Rock Prelude, A Radical Rock Stars Prequel - Book 0.5
Go back to the beginning where it all began and see how Tommy & Jessi fall in love in this prequel to The Prince of Punk Rock!

Tommy Blade is a rock star on the rise—and he has a secret. A secret he has no intention of sharing with anyone.

Jessi Armstrong craves fun and excitement and has big dreams of becoming the next sought-after fashion designer.

Their perfect storybook romance is shattered when Jessi realizes that Tommy is hiding something, and she knows exactly what it is. Unsure how to move forward, she goes on as if nothing has changed, even though unanswered questions and uncertainty about their future plague her heart. It takes a sexy dream to open her mind to things she never imagined she'd be into, and it just may be the salvation she needs.

This full-length novel is a prequel to The Prince of Punk Rock, Radical Rock Stars Book 1 and can be read as a stand-alone. While The Prince of Punk Rock ends in a polyamorous relationship, this book is strictly mf.

Jenna Galicki

Praise for The Radical Rock Stars series:

"The Prince of Punk is one smoking hot rock and roll fantasy where the boy gets everything he ever wanted - a hot wife, a hot boyfriend and a hot band playing sold out venues." ~ Kindle Crack Book Reviews

"...racy, hot filled with fury...From love to hatred, from peace to turbulence...I could almost see it happening on the big screen." ~ Adriana LG "L.A.N.G."

"…mesmorising, unputdownable and exhausting - but SO worth it. . .Stunning." ~ Wicked Reads Team

"Crazy writing and reading at its best...I loved it." ~ Wicked Reads Team

"This book was just heart wrenching. The emotional roller coaster all of the characters go through was almost more than I could take." ~ Jodie's W.I.N.E. List

"Jenna Galicki gives us a scorching hot romance . . . Ms. Galicki doesn't hold back and gives us the gritty lows as well as the highs." ~ Illustrious Illusions

Radical Rock Stars Next Generation

The progeny of legendary punk rock band Immortal Angel brings you a friends-to-lovers and enemies-to-lovers duet.

LUCAS BLADE, Duet Book 1 (Enemies to Lovers)

He's the son of guitar legend, Tommy Blade. He's smart. He's gorgeous. He's talented beyond belief. He's perfect. And he knows it. He's also giving me the opportunity of a lifetime. He's trying to teach me his wisdom, but I just want to play music. He's so damn confident and self-assured it makes me crazy. He's also breaking through all of my barriers.

She's a spitfire. She's got a smart mouth and an answer for everything. I'm trying to help her, but she's fighting me every step of the way. She challenges me, something no one has ever done before. I can't stand her, but I can't stop thinking about her, either.

Lucas Blade was born into a world of extravagance.
Sindy Cavanaugh can barely afford to pay for necessities.
He has a close and loving family who support him.
She has dysfunctional parents who only call her for money.
Their backgrounds couldn't be more different, but music brought them together.
From the moment they meet, they challenge one another with defiant attitudes and oversized egos, and their constant arguing disrupts rehearsals. They come to realize that the turbulence between them is really only a guise for suppressed passion. With their band about to go mainstream, they need to figure out if they should put their feelings on hold or risk everything they've worked toward.

MASON WILDER, Duet Book 2 (Friends to Lovers)
She's my best friend's little sister. She's off limits. She's Tessa Blade Garcia, a girl who knows what she wants and isn't afraid to go after it. And now she's after me.

Everything in my life has had a predetermined path. The success of the band had to come first. I've put my feelings on hold long enough. The time is finally right. Mason Wilder is America's most eligible rock star. Now, I'm going to make him mine.

I've known her since the day she was born, but it's taken me 22 years to realize how much I love her. Just when everything seems perfect, my world gets turned upside down, and I need to take sides between people I've loved and trusted my entire life, and someone I never thought I'd see again.

Jenna Galicki

BLADE, A Sports Romance

Hot jock meets sexy doctor with daddy issues and a secret past. What could go wrong? Everything.

He's the all-American athlete and every woman's dream, including mine. But he could end up being my worst nightmare.

I've worked with professional athletes for my entire career, vowing never to cross the line of the doctor/patient relationship—until Robert Blade walks into my practice. He's my secret crush. My kryptonite. The hunky, blond-haired, blue-eyed offensive lineman with the perpetual smile could be the one person to make me break an oath I've sworn to for years. He could also expose everything and destroy what's left of my family.

The last thing I need is to be sidelined by an injury at the beginning of the NFL season. Enter Dr. A.C. Morgan, New Jersey's top Doctor of Physical Therapy. Her credentials are impressive and impeccable, just like her appearance. But there's something familiar behind those sexy librarian glasses and under the neat bun at the nape of her neck. And I'd recognize those sweetheart lips anywhere. I know exactly who she is— or do I?

This stand-alone sports romance is a spin-off from the Radical Rock Stars series. Robert Blade is Tommy Blade's brother and featured as a side character in several of the books in that series.

BLADE
JENNA GALICKI

Jealousy, a stand-alone novel

Is it possible to love someone of the opposite sex without being in love? Did you ever wonder what it was like to have a soulmate who wasn't your lover? Find out in Jealousy. Two best friends, a straight woman and a gay man, struggle to find someone to love as much as they love each other.

He's the shoulder she leans on.
He worships her.
She shields and protects him.
He watches over her.
They're soul mates for life.
They're not lovers; they're best friends.
Their struggle to find someone who can handle their intense bond is met with a roller coaster of raw emotion, loyalty and heartache.

Follow their journey to find love.

In this unique read, the reader gets two separate romances Heather's (m/f) and Justin's (m/m) and their friendship, which is the real romance.

When Heather Cooper married Peter, she thought that she had finally found someone who could handle the inseparable bond she shares with her gay best friend, Justin Perrotta. It's only a matter of time, however, before jealousy rears its ugly head and Peter's true feelings emerge. He starts drinking and his erratic behavior threatens their marriage.

Burned by an ex-boyfriend, Justin refuses to open his heart to love again. Wild relationships and one-night stands leave him lonely and unfulfilled, even though he will not admit it. He finds love when he least expects it, but his fear of commitment threatens to ruin the best thing that has ever happened to him.

Praise for Jealousy:

"I fell head over heels in love with the story and the characters. This is a book that I will read again. The friendship between Heather and Justin is stunningly breathtaking." – Book Happiness

"There were highs and lows, laughter and tears, it was an emotional experience I'm glad I chose to follow through with. There was virtually NO predictability." – Happily Ever Chapter

"The story just jumps right off the page at you. Author has out done herself with this book." - Amazon Reader

"What a wonderful read! I loved it and loved how it ended! Brilliantly done!" – The Book Obsessed Momma

"I love a book that sends me on an emotional roller-coaster ride! Anger, frustration, joy, sadness, shock! This book had it all!" – Amazon Reader

"Jenna Galicki perfectly captures what it is to be someone's soul mate without being their lover. There is such beauty and brutal truth in the relationship depicted between Heather and Justin." – Amazon Reader

"Not only are the characters compelling and vivid, the plot twists, unexpected turns and the sheer velocity of the lives these characters live is breath taking." – Amazon Reader

"Jealousy is a deep story that is fun, sexy, and has just enough twists that when you think you have something figured out, it changes." – Illustrious Illusions

Jealousy
JENNA GALICKI

Sample: The Stage (Radical Rock Stars Book 6) – Immortal Angel meets Bulletproof!

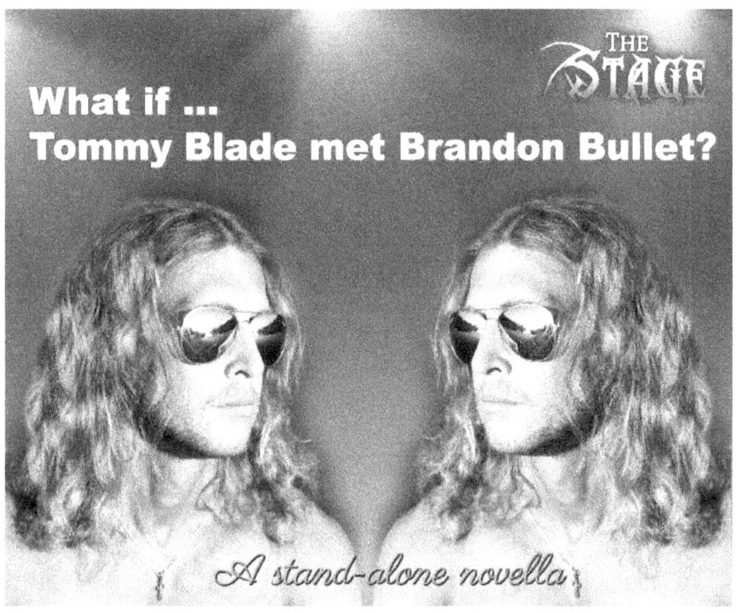

Even rock stars get starstruck. Meeting heavy metal icon Brandon Bullet is a dream come true for Tommy Blade. When Immortal Angel decides to add Tommy's rock star idol as a guest singer to their set at the Get Rocked Festival, sparks fly and egos collide.

Angel Garcia, Immortal Angel's flashy frontman, isn't happy about sharing the spotlight or Tommy's attention. That all changes once Angel has a mind-blowing rehearsal with the charismatic lead singer of Bulletproof.

The sexual chemistry on stage between Angel and Brandon is something Tommy never counted on. Now he's forced to watch his husband and his idol strut on stage together and share a connection that, up until now, only he and Angel shared. The guest appearance by Tommy's rock star idol just lost most of its appeal.
Commissioned to design custom-made rock and roll attire, even Angel and Tommy's wife Jessi gets one-on-one time with Brandon Bullet.

Taking a back seat wasn't on the agenda. Add Angel and Brandon's secret rehearsals together, and Tommy is left in the shadows wondering exactly what's going on between the two.

Like everything else in Tommy's life, it all unfolds on stage.

Epilogue by Brandon Bullet of Bulletproof.

Sample:

Tommy had no clue what winning throws of the dice were, but everyone was cheering wildly, and his chips doubled, then tripled.

Brandon raised a finger, and a waitress was at his side in a matter of seconds. She returned with a tray of shot glasses and an ice bucket filled with open beer bottles.

"What is this?" Tommy asked, taking a shot glass from the tray.

"Just a little Jack Daniels. We have to toast our new friendship." Brandon raised his glass. "To rock and roll, baby!"

"To rock and roll." Tommy winced as the alcohol burned his throat.

Angel was staring at his empty glass, licking his lips. "That was delicious. I never drink liquor. That really hit the spot."

Tommy crinkled his brows. Hit the spot? Angel never drank anything harsh in order to protect his delicate vocal cords, and the liquor tasted like gasoline. "You're acting a little weird tonight. You OK?"

"Perfectly fine, mi amor."

"Hey, Tommy." Derek got his attention. "You know what would be really cool? If you and me dueled axes. I'd love to throw down with you, bruh. It's kind of a dream of mine."

Playing guitar with me was Derek MacAlister's dream? Floored by the compliment, Tommy almost wrapped his arms around the guy. "That would be fucking awesome. What if you and Brandon made a surprise guest appearance during our set?"

"That'd be fuckin' wicked!"

"I'd love to sing with you, Angel, if you don't mind," Brandon said. "I know my voice is usually gravelly and deep, but I got range. I think we could work out an edgy harmony that would be really cool."

"That sounds wonderful," Angel replied. "I haven't used my lower register in a long time. I'm looking forward to the challenge of sharing vocals." He picked up another shot of Jack Daniels and drained it.

Tommy was on top of the world. He was officially star-struck, and he imagined this was how fans felt when they met him and the rest of Immortal Angel. He was euphoric. He was high on the company around him. He was excited that Brandon and Derek liked him and honored that they respected him as a musician. Sharing casual conversation with them about music and their personal lives was exhilarating. Joining forces on stage would be incredible.

A wooden stick scraped across the table and confiscated about three hundred dollars of Tommy's chips. He was so amped that he didn't even care.

Since the winning streak at the craps table came to an end, Brandon proclaimed it was time to head outside to smoke.

"We're smoking now?" Angel asked Tommy.

"Maybe." Tommy wore a mischievous smile. The guys from Bulletproof made him feel adventurous and made him want to try new things.

Once outside, Brandon's phone went off, and he stepped away from the group while Derek produced a fat joint, lit the end and took several hefty tokes, which engulfed him in a plume of smoke.

Angel wore a disapproving scowl, which Tommy found adorable. The guy was so damn serious all the time. "Lighten up, A. I'm not getting high. I'm just hanging out."

Angel's features softened and his mouth curled into a smile. "I like that plan."

"Cam!" Derek exclaimed. "You made it!"

Tommy stretched his neck, passed Derek, to Brandon who was heading toward them with his arm possessively draped around a well-dressed handsome man, obviously the boyfriend.

After a round of welcoming pats on the back from Brandon's bandmates, Brandon introduced his boyfriend to Tommy and Angel. "These two dudes are in an awesome punk rock band," Brandon said. "That's Tommy Blade, one of the best guitarists in the world, and his husband Angel Garcia, an iconic singer and showman. This is my guy, Cam."

Tommy was flabbergasted at the introduction, and his ego inflated to twice its size.

"Musicians? I would have never guessed." Cam smiled a gorgeous white smile. "Nice meeting you guys." He extended his hand, which Tommy and Angel shook.

"Likewise," Angel replied.

"Great to meet you. Brandon was just talking about you," Tommy said.

"I got here as soon as I could. I drove from L.A. Traffic was a mess." Cam waved his arm to dissipate some of the pot smoke that drifted in front of his face. "Put that thing out!" he told Derek "You're gonna get us arrested."

"You're no fun, bruh." Derek snubbed out the joint on the side of the building and stuffed it into his pocket.

"He's lots of fun," Brandon corrected. "He brought the good stuff."

Tommy and Angel glanced at one another, wondering what "the good stuff" could be.

Cam pulled a small pouch from the inside pocket of his jacket and opened it. "Fresh out of the humidor."

They were cigars.

Jeremy and Alan both reached for the pouch at the same time, but Cam pulled it away. "My man gets first dibs."

Brandon lovingly nuzzled his face into Cam's neck and took a cigar. He ran it under his nose and inhaled deeply. "*Ahh*. You'd have to go to Cuba to get something better than this."

After offering the cigars to Alan and Jeremy, Cam offered them to Tommy and Angel.

Angel grinned as he helped himself to a cigar and Cam produced a lighter. "My uncle brings the real thing from Havana all the time."

"No shit?" Brandon raised his brow, impressed.

"Yes. Among other things." Angel pushed his chest out, leaned his head back and puffed on the cigar like Fidel Castro, sending a cone of smoke several feet into the air.

Tommy stifled a laugh. Enjoying a good cigar was one thing, smoking it like a dying man sucking on an oxygen mask was something totally different. This, plus the drinking, had Tommy baffled. "Take it easy, A. You have to sing this weekend."

"I think my throat can handle a little smoke and alcohol, mi amor. But I do appreciate your concern."

Derek wrapped his arm around Brandon's neck. "Maybe Mr. Close-The-Door-I'm-Getting-A-Draft-On-My-Throat can share some of his special remedies."

Brandon's face perked up. "There's a great herbal tea that—"

The arm Derek had around Brandon's neck turned into a playful headlock, cutting off Brandon's sentence. "I was joking," Derek said. "No one wants to hear about your herbal tea!"

Brandon laughed and shoved his friend away. "You're a riot. Go break up those two before someone gets hurt." He was referring to Jeremy and Alan, who were roughhousing next to a row of cars.

These guys were all about having a good time. Always joking around and play fighting. Watching them made Tommy feel like a teenager again, and he had the urge to tackle Angel, a throwback from Tommy's football days.

"What other goodies do you bring back from Cuba?" Brandon asked Angel.

"Coffee. Rum. But I haven't been to Cuba since I was a little boy. My uncle brings them with him when he visits."

"Which is all the time," Tommy quickly added. "We get this great sugar too. It's like brown sugar or raw sugar, but it's not. It tastes different. Like toffee. What's it called, A?"

"Demerara."

"I like sugar." Brandon placed his arm around Tommy's shoulder. "Rum. Cigars. Sugar. Your place sounds awesome."

"We got a full recording studio too." Tommy couldn't help bragging. He loved that Brandon seemed fascinated by *him*.

Brandon jerked his head back. "Woah. That's rad. I'm definitely gonna hit you up the next time I'm in New York."

"Yes." Angel smiled, but in a weird way. "We'll drink rum, smoke cigars, eat sugar, and record a song."

A car alarm blared as Alan and Jeremy, who still hadn't stopped roughhousing, fell into a Lexus.

"Let's go back inside," Brandon called to the rest of the guys, who were all inspecting the car for damage. "You ready?" he asked Tommy.

"Shit yeah. Let's throw some more money down on the craps table."

Brandon pulled the cigar from his mouth and smiled. "You're all right, bruh." He held up his hand for a bro-shake, which Tommy slapped as he grabbed it.

"You too man." This was turning out to be one of the best nights of Tommy's life.

Jenna Galicki

Sample: The Prince of Punk Rock, (Radical Rock Stars Book 1)
I love *her*, but I also love *him*.
She's everything to me.
He sets my world on fire.
It's our dirty little secret, and it's about to blow our record deal sky high.
I'm Tommy Blade, the Prince of Punk Rock, and this is our story.

Tommy Blade is a man with a secret. It's a secret he only shares with one person, Jessi Blade – and the men he surrenders to in the bedroom. Jessi's only condition to their tumultuous sex life is that these men are one-night stands. But when Angel Garcia enters Tommy's life, it's like a match to gasoline.

Mega-talented punk rock singer Angel Garcia, with his smoldering ebony eyes, tight leather pants and unstoppable stage presence, is a man who is used to getting what he wants. He has his eyes set on Tommy Blade as his new lead guitarist, and as his life partner.

Jessi Blade, sympathetic to her husband's bisexual needs, loves him enough to share him, but she never counted on Angel Garcia to test the threshold of her marriage. He makes her life hell . . . and heaven. He's her damnation and her salvation. She wants to hate him. She wants to despise him. But his charm and raw sex appeal are impossible to resist. Without warning, she finds herself falling in love with her husband's gay lover.

At the height of it all, their punk rock band catapults to stardom.

Their lives are marred by secrecy, deception and sacrifice. Feelings of betrayal, backlash from the sensationalistic media and threats of blackmail send them down a hard road filled with tough decisions.

They aren't your ordinary rock stars. They're radical rock stars. And they have a big story to tell.

CHAPTER ONE

"Let's just get one thing straight. If it gets weird for either of us, we stop. We throw this guy out of our bed. No questions asked. No explanations. Agreed?"

Jessi nodded, eagerly. "Agreed."

That's how it all started, two hours ago.

Tommy Blade hadn't been with a man in a long time – too long – not since he met Jessi, over a year ago. He never thought he would confess his secret desires to anyone, but Jessi wasn't just anyone. It didn't matter that the hard muscles of a man's body made his mouth water, or that the scent of a slightly sweaty man made him dizzy with excitement, he wanted to spend the rest of his life with Jessi.

He still struggled with the truth. He still couldn't find the courage to say the words out loud, but Jessi knew. She always knew what was going on in his head. They often shared silent gazes that transcended the spoken word. It was a connection that few people shared.

Tommy was forced to trust Jessi or else he risked losing her. He was determined to make her his wife, even if it meant letting her see a side of him that he swore he would never let anyone see. It was a side he kept tucked away, hidden from the world, brought to life only during the brief encounters with the men he surrendered to in the bedroom.

When Tommy met Jessi, he tried to forget about his obsession, but the broad chest of a handsome man always turned his head and made his insides yearn for physical contact. The soft stubble against his cheek, the force behind a man's kiss and the strength of a man's hand on his body, were all things that sent his heart racing. Exercising restraint was tough, but Tommy never acted on his desires. Not since he met Jessi. Not until tonight.

The threesome was Jessi's idea. She simply presented it as a viable solution for the both of them to find sexual fulfillment and let the scenario fester in his head. At first, he opposed the idea, but the scenario quickly ballooned into a full-length erotic fantasy that he couldn't suppress.

He went to a gay bar, two towns away. It was the same pick-up joint he frequented before he met Jessi. Its discreet location provided camouflage and anonymity. From the outside it looked like an unoccupied building. The windows were blackened out. There was no name displayed on the establishment to introduce itself to the world. If the place had a name, it was never spoken. It was an underground club and invitation was strictly by word of mouth.

The faces changed since the last time he was there, but the intention was still the same. It wasn't a place to socialize or partake in camaraderie or drop in for a drink on your way home. It was a meeting place for men interested in casual sex. The backroom served as a shanty for a quick encounter. You could stop in, get your rocks off and be on your way in half an hour. It was a smorgasbord of testosterone, a buffet of muscle and beefcake.

Tommy got hard the minute he laid eyes on the place. He knew the secrets that transpired behind the façade of the ordinary-looking building. Men flocked around him as soon as he walked through the door. They always did. A guy once told him that it was the mixture of his rugged jaw and strong upper body, offset by the innocence of his big blue eyes that made him so attractive. The ladies always said it was his long blond hair and the guitar.

It didn't take Tommy long to pick someone he wanted to bring home. Less than an hour later, the three of them were in his bedroom. He still couldn't believe they really went through with it.

Tommy never expected Jessi to get off watching him with another man . . . watching him get rammed in the ass by a total stranger . . . rammed so perfectly in the ass . . . rammed so deep that it felt like a cock was about to touch the back of his throat from the opposite end. But she did.

Now that it was over, and they were alone, there was silence. He waited for Jessi to say something. Anything. Each muted second that passed made his cheeks flush hotter. When Jessi finally turned to look at him, she had a mischievous spark in her eyes. She leaned closer to him, looked straight at him and said, "That was the hottest fuckin' thing I've ever done."

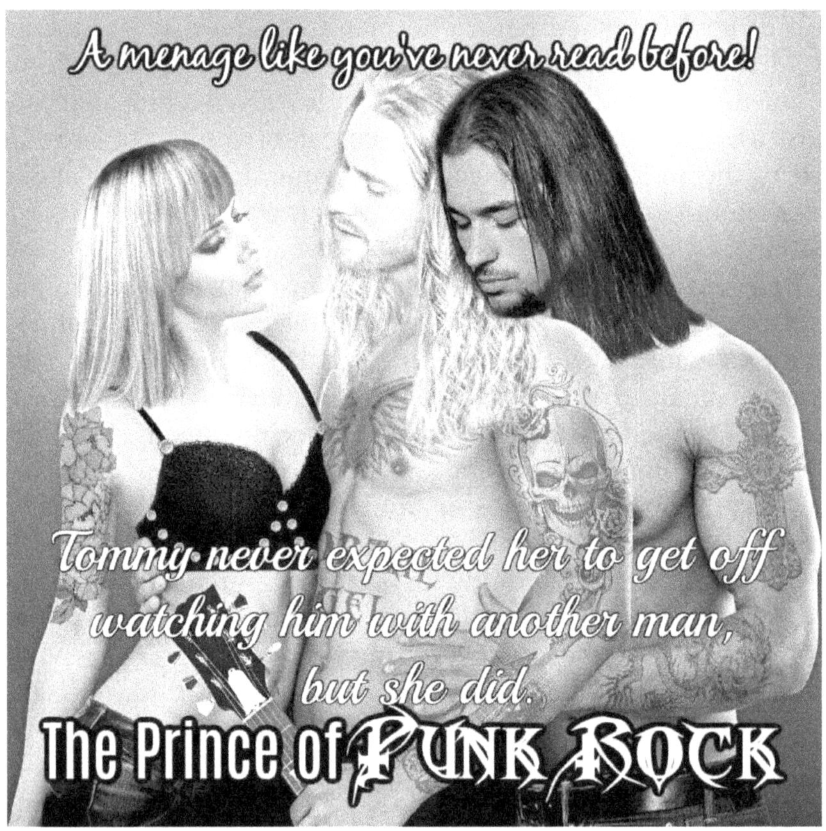

Jenna Galicki

About the Author:

Jenna Galicki writes in multiple genres including mm, mmf and mf. The Prince of Punk Rock (Radical Rock Stars Book 1) was a finalist in the 2015 Bisexual Book Awards.

A native New Yorker, she now resides in Southern California. She's a Rottweiler enthusiast and an avid music buff. When she's not hunched over a computer, you can find her front row at a rock concert.

Follow Jenna, she would love to hear from you:

www.jennagalicki.com
Facebook
Facebook reader group: Jenna Galicki's Rock Stars
Amazon
Instagram
BookBub
Goodreads
Twitter

Jenna Galicki